Protector

Anna Hackett

Protector

Published by Anna Hackett
Copyright 2017 by Anna Hackett
Cover by Melody Simmons of eBookindiecovers
Edits by Tanya Saari

ISBN (eBook): 978-1-925539-15-8
ISBN (paperback): 978-1-925539-16-5

This book is a work of fiction. All names, characters, places and incidents are either the product of the author's imagination or are used fictitiously. Any resemblance to actual persons, events or places is coincidental. No part of this book may be reproduced, scanned, or distributed in any printed or electronic form.

What readers are saying about Anna's Science Fiction Romance

Galactic Gladiators — Most Original Story Universe Winner 2016 — Gravetells

Gladiator — Two-time winner for Best Sci-fi Romance 2016 — Gravetells and Under the Covers

Hell Squad — Amazon Bestselling Science Fiction Romance Series and SFR Galaxy Award for best Post-Apocalypse for Readers who don't like Post-Apocalypse

At Star's End — One of Library Journal's Best E-Original Romances for 2014

Return to Dark Earth — One of Library Journal's Best E-Original Books for 2015 and two-time SFR Galaxy Awards winner

The Phoenix Adventures — SFR Galaxy Award Winner for Most Fun New Series and "Why Isn't This a Movie?" Series

Beneath a Trojan Moon — RWAus Ella Award Winner for Romantic Novella of the Year

"Like Indiana Jones meets Star Wars. A treasure hunt with a steamy romance." – SFF Dragon, review of *Among Galactic Ruins*

"Strap in, enjoy the heat of romance and the daring of this group of space travellers!" – Di, Top 500 Amazon Reviewer, review of *At Star's End*

"High action and adventure surrounding an impossible treasure hunt kept me reading until late in the night." – Jen, That's What I'm Talking About, review of *Beyond Galaxy's Edge*

"Action, danger, aliens, romance – yup, it's another great book from Anna Hackett!" – Book Gannet Reviews, review of *Hell Squad: Marcus*

Don't miss out! For updates about new releases, action romance info, free books, and other fun stuff, sign up for my VIP mailing list and get your *free box set* containing three action-packed romances.

Visit here to get started:
www.annahackettbooks.com

Chapter One

She desperately wanted to be anywhere else but here.

Madeline Cochran turned slowly, studying all the party guests around her. They were laughing, sipping drinks, and having a good time. And they were all aliens.

She picked at the plate of food in her hand. She was still adjusting to the different foods and strange flavors on the world of Carthago. Nothing looked even remotely familiar. Her stomach lurched, and she set the plate down.

As she moved, her dress swished around her. Madeline had rarely worn long dresses—she preferred her suits—so the sensation of the soft fabric on her legs, and the air gently brushing the shoulders the dress left bare, heightened the feeling of not belonging.

Here she was, at a post-gladiatorial fight party on a planet thousands of light-years away from home, struggling to accept the fact that she had no way back to Earth.

A passing server held out a tray and she grabbed a tall glass. Her fingers tightened on the drink, which was filled with some blue liquid that tasted a lot like wine. All around her, the room was filled with people who towered over her. Alien gladiators, of all things. Everywhere she turned, she saw muscled, bare chests, leather, and metal. And scattered among the giant men were scantily-dressed women, laughing loudly.

A giant alien with thick, brown skin walked past Madeline. Instantly, memories hammered into her. Her pulse tripped, her heart beating hard in her chest. That alien's color, its skin, reminded her of the Thraxians who'd abducted her from her space station that had been orbiting Jupiter.

She'd been a prisoner, drugged for most of her captivity, and torn from her home. From her son.

Madeline quickly gulped some of her drink. It burned all the way down, and settled uncomfortably in her stomach. She'd been rescued by some other human women from her station who'd survived the attack, and by the big, tough gladiators from the House of Galen.

She turned again, her gaze raking the room and all the different kinds of aliens in it. The sound seemed to get louder, the lights brighter. Suddenly, her chest went tight. She couldn't breathe. She needed to get out of here.

Stumbling through the crowd, she set her glass down blindly and made her way toward the glass door leading to the balcony. Her breathing turned raspy. She shoved her way out into the warm night.

She hurried into the shadows and leaned against the railing. As her hands curled on the stone, she tried to slow her panicked breathing.

She was Madeline Cochran. She did *not* panic.

Down below her lay the now-empty arena, wreathed in darkness. Earlier today, she'd watched the gladiators fighting each other on the sand. It had been a mind-blowing display of power, skill, and brutality. She still wasn't sure how she felt about it.

Her gaze moved upward to the large moon that hung in the sky. Another reminder that she was on an alien planet, far from Earth. She pressed a hand to her churning stomach. Nothing reminded her of home.

Sadness clogged her throat as she thought of Jack. Her son was sixteen years old and on the verge of becoming a man. Her stomach started to churn harder.

Madeline had come from nothing, grown up dirt poor with an alcoholic mother, and she'd been going nowhere, fast. Then, at eighteen, she'd fallen pregnant.

At first, Madeline had thought her life was over, until that baby had been placed in her arms. Jack had been all chubby rolls, with an angry, red face. He'd changed everything. She'd gone from a directionless teenager to a focused woman.

She imagined his face, the strong lines of it hinting at the man he'd become. Tears pricked her eyes, but she fought them back. She'd broken down and sobbed once after her rescue from the Thraxians, but never again. Tears never solved anything, and she hated the show of weakness.

But the thought of never seeing her son again...

No. Madeline straightened her shoulders. One way or another, she'd hear Jack's voice again.

"Hiding?"

The liquid-smooth voice held the hint of a smile. Madeline recognized it instantly. She stiffened, and slowly turned her head.

Lore Uma-Xilene stood just inches away. Like all gladiators, he was tall and strong. A little leaner than the others from the House of Galen, with long, tawny hair that brushed his shoulders, and a distracting bare chest. She tried to calm her nerves, but something about this alien gladiator made her nervous. Madeline didn't do nervous.

Okay, maybe she was just embarrassed that he'd seen her at her worst: drugged out of her mind and weak. He'd been the one to carry her out of the underground fight rings where the Thraxians and their allies, the Srinar, had kept her. She'd clung to him like some crushed damsel.

She'd watched him battle this evening. He was a flashy fighter, who loved to wow the crowd with illusions and tricks. The spectators loved him for it, and women threw themselves at him.

Looking up, her gaze snagged on his long-boned face and silver eyes that gleamed in the darkness.

"Don't you have women to charm?" She'd seen him surrounded by a gaggle of women—arena flutterers the others called them—at the party.

He gave her a slow smile, his teeth white in the darkness. "Yes, I do." His gaze was heavy on her.

Silence hung between them, and Madeline hunched her shoulders. "It's wasted on me."

He rested his elbows on the railing, looking down toward the tiers of empty seats in the arena. "Beautiful woman. Beautiful night. That's not wasted to me."

As he leaned farther forward, she watched the flex of muscles in his strong arms. She couldn't deny that the man had a gorgeous body and was very easy to look at.

Madeline forced herself to glance away. "Look, I'm not the weak, malleable woman you rescued. I'm sorry if you're confused, because I clung to you—"

"Because you needed to be held and comforted after a bad situation."

She huffed out a breath and looked at him again. "I'm not your type, Lore, and you're certainly not mine."

Lore arched a brow. "You looked like you needed a friend. That's why I followed you out here."

He reached out, and Madeline forced herself to stay still. His fingers brushed the shell of her ear, and with a flourish, he held out his hand. He was holding a beautiful, white flower that he'd conjured out of thin air.

The blossom was stunning, giving off a fragrant perfume. She itched to touch it.

Instead, she clenched her fingers in the folds of her dress. "I don't have friends. I have work." Or at least, she used to have work. That was all gone now. Her gut cramped. God, she hoped those who hadn't made it off the space station hadn't suffered.

She'd been the station commander, and in

charge of their well-being. And she'd failed them.

Her thoughts snapped back to her son. *Please be okay, Jack.*

A sharp pain stabbed through her stomach, and she gasped, pressing her hand to the railing to steady herself.

Lore frowned, his silver gaze like a laser on her face. "What's wrong?"

"Nothing. I'm not your concern. Or your friend."

She put on her best bitch voice. She'd honed it to perfection during her career in a male-dominated company.

Lore shook his head. "Such sadness in your eyes, Madeline. I know the situation isn't what you wanted, but real strength is how you cope with the things you didn't want or plan for."

His words made the hot press of tears sting her eyes again. No, strength was standing on your own two feet and not breaking. She'd never let herself lean on somebody else.

When you depended on another person, they always let you down.

No, she wouldn't let herself weaken, even for this tempting man.

***

So prickly. Lore had been raised by women, among women. He'd been brought up to love them, respect them, and protect them. It didn't matter their shapes or sizes—or temperament—he found them all fascinating.

PROTECTOR

He smiled a little to himself. As one of the few males born into a matriarchal family, he'd been spoiled and indulged. He remembered when he'd wanted a pet *dragmata* lizard. He'd pleaded with his mother over and over until she'd finally relented. He'd petted that thorny-skinned, bad-tempered creature until his fingers bled and his arms were covered in bites.

Until it had loved him back.

He'd always loved a challenge. Now, he looked into sad blue eyes. Those eyes tempted him, too. He knew what it was like to be ripped from your life and lose those you loved. He knew what it was to lose everything.

He wanted to tell Madeline that the hole in her heart would never go away, but that time would fill around it with other things...if she let it.

But he knew she wasn't ready yet. She'd only been here two weeks, and before that had suffered for months at the hands of the Thraxians.

Lore had watched her inside at the party. She hadn't eaten much, and was edgy and tense. He knew that wouldn't help with her recovery.

"Any word on Blaine?" she asked. "Or the underground fight rings?"

He saw her desperate need to change the subject, although he wished she'd picked a better one. The thoughts of the underground fight rings run by the Srinar left a bad taste in his mouth. He had tried his best to forget everything about that rotten place, where he and the other gladiators of the House of Galen had rescued Madeline.

Unfortunately, on the same mission, they'd spotted another human from Earth, Blaine Strong, but hadn't been able to rescue him. He was still down there, somewhere, fighting for his life in the vicious fight rings. If he was still alive, that was...

Up here, the gladiatorial fights in the arena were a wild, brutal show for the masses. People came from all over the occupied systems, and paid a lot of money to watch the gladiators fight. Many stayed on to spend more on all the delights offered in the hedonistic District—casinos, brothels, restaurants, and shows.

The gladiators were a strange mix. Some were sold into slavery to the Kor Magna Arena and fought to earn their freedom; some came willingly to hone their fighting skills. Most left as fast as starships could carry them, but some, like him, earned their freedom and made a home here, instead.

However, the arena battles were never fights to the death. Gladiators were big investments for the Houses who fed them, trained them, and healed them. It was a different story in the hidden, underground world in the bowels under the arena. There, in the illegal fight rings, stolen fighters were forced to fight to the death.

"Galen says all known entrances to the fight rings have been closed down. They've been blocked off, or filled up. No invites are being issued to spectators, either."

He saw a muscle tick in the side of Madeline's face.

Lore continued. "Our contact, Zhim—"

She straightened. "The information merchant."

"Yes. Anything worth knowing on Carthago, Zhim knows. And he'll sell it, for a price."

"You think that the Srinar have closed the fight rings?"

Lore considered lying, and making it easier for her. But something told him that a woman like Madeline Cochran wouldn't appreciate lies, no matter how pretty they were.

"No. They've just gone deeper. The Srinar have gotten more careful and better at hiding. The underground fight rings are too profitable for them to shut down."

She let out a breath. "So, Blaine is still fighting for his life."

Lore felt a stab of pity for the man. Fighting to the death just to survive. What would that do to a man's soul?

"I have to find him." Fire ignited in Madeline's eyes, mixed with a healthy dose of stubbornness.

Lore liked seeing it. He'd take anger over the sadness that had been drowning in her eyes before.

He turned his head a little and looked back through the doorway into the party. His fellow gladiators were having a great time. He saw tattoo-covered Raiden with his trademark red cloak, and by his side another woman of Earth, Harper. Her friend Rory was beside her, laughing, her unique, flame-colored hair a riot around her face. Behind Rory, her lover Kace stood tall and alert.

When the women spotted Lore and Madeline,

they waved madly, gesturing for them to come inside.

"Your friends are calling you," he said.

Indecision flitted over Madeline's face. "They're not my friends. They weren't before."

Lore smiled and offered her his arm. "I think they are now, whether you like it or not."

She reluctantly put her arm in his and he led her toward the door. Their bodies brushed together and he felt a lick of heat. He wondered why she appealed to him so much, but he decided to just enjoy it. Feeling mischievous, he purposely brushed against her again, slipping the bloom he'd gotten for her into tiny rope belted around her waist.

She instantly put some space between them. "Back off."

"I seem to have trouble doing that. A minute with you is far more interesting than an hour in that party, especially when I seem to irritate you so easily."

She scowled. "I don't like you."

"Fair enough, but you don't really know me. And I'm not entirely sure I like you, either."

"Are you always this reasonable?" she muttered.

"Mostly."

They took another step and as Lore reached for the door, she hissed and stumbled. She pressed a hand to her stomach.

He frowned. "What is it?"

She straightened. "Nothing. Just something I ate." She pushed past him to head inside.

She'd barely eaten anything. Lore followed more

slowly. He loved women, and more than anything, he was a sucker for a damsel in distress.

He watched the sway of Madeline's hips under her white dress as she walked away. Yes, a complete pushover for a sexy, beautiful damsel. Not that Madeline would appreciate the title.

Chapter Two

Madeline slipped the books back onto the shelf in a neat order. Most of them had been left in haphazard piles on the nearby desk. All the books were in different alien languages that she couldn't read. The implant she'd been given by the Thraxians meant she could speak and understand various alien languages, but she couldn't read them.

She turned, studying the chest of drawers in the corner that was overflowing, and clearly lacking any sort of organization. She grabbed the notepad she'd had Rory find for her, and started scrawling some notes. She had several ideas for a better filing system, and, after that, she was going to start work on improving inventory for the kitchen and cleaning staff. Over the last few weeks, she'd studied everything the workers at the House of Galen did. The imperator ensured things ran smoothly in his house, but she knew they were overstocked in some things, and understocked in others. She could certainly make it more efficient.

Madeline paused for a second, looking around the spacious office, gaze skating over the now-organized bookshelves. She liked making things fit, making things flow more efficiently. It made her feel productive, like she'd accomplished something.

She'd grown up in a rat-infested apartment in the outer suburbs of Los Angeles, always being slapped down and told she'd never amount to anything. Never be smart enough, good enough, or clever enough. Her mother had been a hard, bitter woman who'd loved the bottle more than her daughter. For a very long time, Madeline had believed her.

But when life had forced Madeline to grow up, she'd realized that her life was in her hands. It was the actions she took that made a difference.

She finished making notes, and picked up some papers for filing. She knew they had an electronic system as well, and made a mental note to get access and take a look at it. As she slid the papers into the file drawers, she heard male voices outside the office. She straightened and turned.

The Imperator of the House of Galen stepped inside. Galen was an intimidating man with a big, muscled form and an air of authority. That he was a few years older than his gladiators didn't diminish his power at all, only enhanced it. His tough face was scarred, and one eye was covered by a black eye-patch. The other eye was a glittering ice-blue.

Right behind him were Raiden and Lore. Lore's silver-gray eyes came straight to her, and locked there.

"What are you doing in my office?" Galen demanded.

"The door was open. I'm just tidying up and improving some of your...organization." Or lack of it. She waved at the shelves, then gestured to her notepad. "I also have some ideas for improving the house's inventory of goods for the kitchens, cleaning, and Medical."

As Galen kept staring at her, she felt a trickle of unease, and stiffened her spine.

Lore sauntered forward, and for a second she was caught by the liquid way he moved. Powerful and limber, like he knew exactly how to use his body—to fight, to escape, to pleasure a woman. Madeline choked that thought off.

He perched on the corner of Galen's glossy desk. "It's not your real reason for being here, though, is it?"

She scowled. Why did this man always make her feel like she was wearing a neon sign on her head broadcasting everything she was thinking? "No." She moved her gaze to meet Galen's. "I want to know what's being done to find Blaine."

"I told you that the underground fight rings have gone deeper," Lore said.

"But we all know they're still operational. They're still making him fight." Madeline's voice hitched, and she felt a flutter of panic. She hated losing control.

Galen circled his desk, lowering his powerful body into his chair. His face was its usual impassive mask. For a second, Madeline wondered what the man really felt beneath the controlled front.

"I'm waiting to hear from my contacts," Galen said. "I also have meetings planned with the other gladiator houses that are allied with the House of Galen."

"Meetings?" She frowned. "Why?"

Galen eyed her. "It's in our interests to shut down the fight rings. We don't have a lot of rules here in Kor Magna, but the Srinar and their allies are flaunting the unwritten ones. Plus, the fight rings are luring some of our clientele away."

Madeline knew that wasn't really it. The stands in the arena were packed, night after night. "You're planning to invade the underground fight rings."

Galen lifted one shoulder. "I have to talk with the other imperators first. The House of Galen can't do this alone. Besides, we've already raided the fight rings once. The Srinar and the Thraxians will be watching us."

Madeline released a breath. She hated just hearing the names of the aliens who'd kept her captive. The demon-like, horned Thraxians—worse than any nightmare—and the plague-deformed Srinar. "I'm not very good at waiting. I like action. I want to help. I *need* to help."

Galen didn't move. "Madeline—"

"No. The Thraxians pumped me full of drugs, they kept me docile, they beat me. I saw them inject Blaine too. Over and over. But it was different for him...it made him more aggressive. We have to get him out of there."

She watched the three gladiators trade glances.

"We're doing everything we can," Raiden said.

"Blaine is Harper's friend, and I've promised her we'll get him out."

Raiden Tiago struck Madeline as a man who kept his promises. And she'd seen with her own eyes that he was head-over-heels in love with Harper Adams. It wasn't hard to believe that the competent, tough space marine had fallen for this alien gladiator.

"I assure you we are working to free Blaine," Galen said. "For now, we have a large arena fight to plan for. It's a mock sea battle and they draw the biggest crowds. I need my team focused. That includes my gladiators and my back-of-House team who are pulling everything together."

She watched him share another long look with Lore and Raiden and she narrowed her gaze. "You know something else?"

Galen sighed, sinking back in his chair. "Things were far easier around here when I was the sole person in charge. I'm not sure I enjoy people questioning my every decision."

Lore leaned forward, a faint smile dancing on his lips. "Maybe she can help."

Madeline felt anxiety eating at her. She needed to help find Blaine. She needed to do something to take her mind off what had happened to her, and where she was.

"Fine." Galen waved a hand. "Tell her."

"Galen's invited certain people to the arena battle tonight," Raiden said. "He's also encouraged some...side bets."

Lore shifted. "It's all to entice a certain couple to

attend. A man and a woman called Vashto and Cerria. Word is, they bet big in the underground fight rings."

"They're some of its best clientele," Raiden said darkly.

The meaning behind what they were saying clicked into place for her. "If the fight rings are still operational, the biggest gamblers will know where it is."

Lore nodded. "Exactly."

Raiden crossed his arms over his chest. "We can't afford to scare them off. These two are our only lead."

Madeline nodded. "So we lure them to the battle tonight and then see what we can glean from them."

"I've gathered everything I can about this couple," Galen said. "They like excess and nice things. We ply them with their favorite drinks, and we give them a good show. We give them whatever they want—" a scary look crossed Galen's face "—and then we get what we want."

Madeline tilted her head. "You have a party planned for after the fight?"

"Yes. I've hired a box above the arena."

"It'll be the standard affair? Food, drinks, music?"

Galen nodded.

"Let me help." Madeline pressed her palms against Galen's desk. "If this couple like excess, then let's give them a show they've never seen before."

She felt all the men watching her, and unfamiliar nerves filled her belly. She felt like she was back in the early days of her career, fighting to make her ideas heard. She'd carved out a fantastic career for herself, in order to give her son the life he deserved. She'd gotten very used to never being nervous.

"My staff is already planning the party."

"I can enhance it." She saw Lore watching her. "I need to help. I need to do something. Harper fights, Rory fixes things, and Regan invents. *This* is what I do best. I organize and plan." She swallowed, hating the feeling of being so powerless. "I'll work with your catering people and we'll put on a party people will talk about for years."

Silence fell. Galen's gaze was unwavering, and Madeline felt those nerves threatening again. This was important to her. Then she saw Lore wink at her, and something eased inside.

Finally, Galen nodded. "Okay. Do it."

Elation burst inside her. "Thank you." She nodded. "You won't regret it." She'd make sure of it.

"And Madeline?"

She looked into his single eye, the other covered by that coal-black patch.

"I'll organize an office for you…so you stay out of mine."

She fought back a smile. "Thank you." She hurried out of the office and down the hall. As she turned a corner, she narrowly avoided running into Harper.

"Whoa, hold up," Harper said.

Madeline nodded at the woman and spotted Rory and Regan with her. Madeline had to admit, it was still a bit of a shock to see her former security officer, station engineer, and scientist here in this alien place. Regan was wearing a flowing dress, Rory was in slick, black trousers with a bright-green shirt, and Harper was dressed in fighting leathers. Like the gladiator she now was.

"Mads, how you feeling?" Rory asked.

Mads? Madeline swallowed, her gaze straying to the small, robot dog at Rory's feet. Lights blinked along the dog's sleek, gray metal body. The dog tilted its head like it was studying her.

She really didn't know these women that well. She hadn't allowed herself to have friends on the space station, and this whole ordeal had made her realize that she'd let herself go...hard. On Fortuna Station she'd only had her work, and when she'd visited Earth, she'd spent all her time with Jack. She hadn't even dated.

"I'm good." She wasn't going to tell them about her constantly churning stomach and the feeling of never quite belonging. "And you?" Her gaze dropped to Rory's still-flat stomach. Not only had Rory fallen in love with an alien gladiator, she'd gotten herself pregnant by one.

"Wonderful." Rory patted her belly with a smile. "The Hermia healers tell me the little guy is growing just fine." She screwed up her nose. "They're already going into fits about how someone my size can give birth to an Antarian child, but I'm sure they'll have it figured out once this little bump is cooked."

"Except they don't know how long your gestation period will be, exactly," Regan said, her gaze turning inward. Once a scientist always a scientist.

A screwed-up nose again. "They'll figure it out." Rory smiled. "I'm just happy to see my pretty boy turn to mush whenever he touches my belly. He talks to the baby, you know?"

Madeline remembered the amazing sensation of having a child grow inside her. She didn't remember Wade, her ex, ever talking to her belly. But he'd only been one year older than her, and scared spitless about becoming a father.

She cleared her throat. "I just spoke with Galen. I'm going to take over planning the party tonight after the arena sea battle."

"Oh?" Harper said.

"Apparently, he's invited a couple to attend who are known as big betters at the underground fight rings."

Harper straightened. "They think they can find out information from them?"

Madeline nodded. "Apparently, this pair likes a good party."

Rory smiled. "So you're going to give them one, and butter them up."

"That's the plan. And find out where Blaine is."

Regan's pretty face turned worried. "Every time I think of poor Blaine, it makes me feel sick."

Rory pushed her red hair back, her face hardening. "We're getting him back, no matter what it takes."

Madeline nodded. "We won't leave him there."

As a group, they continued down the hall, with its stone-lined walls and gray-and-red wall hangings. The women began to talk about the mock sea battle and party, and kept asking her questions and tossing ideas at her.

Regan reached out and touched Madeline's hair. Instead of her customary bob, it was almost to her shoulders. "You need a haircut. I can organize that for you."

Madeline blinked and managed a nod. They included her so easily. From the day they'd helped rescue her, they'd treated her as a friend. It felt…odd. But now, whether she liked it or not, they were four of only five humans from Earth anywhere in the vicinity of this part of the galaxy. As she listened to Rory and Harper argue over something to do with the arena battle, she realized what a comfort it was to not be completely alone.

The image of silver-gray eyes flashed in her head before she banished it.

Feeling a flare of burning in her belly, Madeline rubbed her stomach. For now, she was going to focus on the party. Just knowing she had something to do made her feel better.

And knowing that she was doing something, anything, to help find Blaine was the best feeling of all.

***

Lore shifted his feet on the sand and swung his sword down.

He moved his blade through powerful arcs and thrusts, his focus narrowed and intense. He thrust the sword forward, the weapon an extension of his body...then he spun in a showy turn.

Of course, here in the House of Galen training arena, there were no spectators to cheer and applaud. Some of the other gladiators refused to pander to the crowd, but Lore figured that they were there for a show, for a spectacle, and he didn't mind giving it to them. He knew why most of those people came to watch the fights. It was the same reason they watched shows, read books, and listened to stories. They were searching for an escape from the reality of their lives, searching for entertainment, inspiration, and feeling.

He lowered his sword. He knew it was almost time for him to go in and prepare for the sea battle. Overhead, the dual suns of Carthago were slowly heading toward the horizon. Soon the arena lights would come on, and spectators would start pouring into the stands.

Hearing movement behind him, he turned, and saw his fight partner Nero stomping in his direction.

Nero was a huge mountain of a man, who came from the barbarian world of Symeria. A planet of extremes from its icy climes in the north, to its steaming jungles at the equator. The man still preferred his fighting leathers rimmed with fur. Nero was a tough fighter, and a man of few words.

Having been his fight partner and his friend for several years, Lore knew Nero was a hunter to the bone. Tracking prey and fighting was in his blood.

Right now, Nero's big form was covered in some fancy metallic armor for tonight's fight. The pattern on the beaten silver metal resembled fish scales, and the armor covered the man's tattooed arms and shoulders, and had a strip across his broad chest. He was scowling, which made his rugged face more threatening.

Lore knew that Nero hated armor. It went against his barbarian nature.

"Looking good, big guy."

Nero made a rude noise. "Came to tell you that you need to get ready. Fight's in under an hour."

"I was about to head in."

Nero grunted. "I suppose you have some tricks up your sleeve for tonight's fight."

"Always." Spectators came to the arena for the show, and Lore liked to make sure they never walked away disappointed.

Over by the arches leading into the House of Galen, Lore spotted Madeline bustling along, talking with some of the kitchen staff. He stared at her, noting that since he'd seen her that morning, she'd changed her hair. Now it was cut off bluntly along her jaw line, the dark strands absorbing the sunlight. It was a businesslike style. He smiled to himself. Or at least she probably thought that. She probably also thought that it hid her femininity.

"I'm not sure I completely understand your interest in that direction," Nero grumbled.

Lore looked back to his friend. "Madeline?"

Nero nodded. "She's...cold, difficult, and broken."

Lore shook his head. "We're all broken somehow, Nero." Lore thought of the family he'd lost so long ago. He'd been twenty, cocky, and thought he had the universe as his playground. Instead, his life had been destroyed, and there were still jagged pieces inside him that hurt. "Besides, she's putting herself back together."

Nero raised a dark brow. "She can be rude and abrasive."

Lore chuckled. "A bit like you?"

His friend crossed his arms over his chest, his scowl deepening. "All I'm saying is I prefer a strong, fun woman looking for some good bed sport. Not one that will lash me with her tongue or freeze me with ice."

"Easy can be fun, my friend," Lore said. "But sometimes the good stuff requires a little effort." He watched Madeline as she walked. She was waving a hand as she described something to one of the chefs. "There's heat there, Nero, but she's locked it up. She's forgotten it's there, and what to do with it."

"So, you're going to help her with that?"

"Yes." The thought of being the one to help Madeline unleash her inner fire made his gut tighten. "I want to be the one to feel the burn."

Nero shook his head. "Sometimes I can't work you out."

Suddenly, Madeline turned her head, and across

the sand of the training arena, their gazes met. Even from this distance, Lore saw the flash of indecision on her face, then she set her shoulders back, waved to the people she was with and headed Lore's way.

"I'm out of here." Nero turned on his heel and stomped away, giving Madeline a brief nod.

"Lore." Madeline reached him. "I was hoping to catch you before the fight."

He spread his arms out. "I'm all yours."

She stared at him for a second, before lifting the papers she held in her hands. "I've changed the party plans a little. I've gone with a bit of a water theme, since water is pretty valued on a desert planet. I'm also planning some entertainment during the party tonight. More than just music." Her blue eyes settled on him. "I know that you like to put on a show."

"Are you asking me to do some illusions at the party?"

She huffed out a breath. "Yes."

"Okay."

"Oh." She relaxed. "Okay, great."

"On one condition."

She turned wary again. "What?"

"You act as my assistant for the show."

"Oh, no." She shook her head. "I organize things behind the scenes, I don't get on stage."

Lore shrugged his shoulders. "Then I won't do it."

A flash of something hot in her eyes. "Lore, I'm not prancing around on a stage—"

"You want to help find your friend, don't you? I need an assistant, and if you won't do it, then there's no show."

"That's blackmail!"

He liked seeing the color rising in her cheeks. "Your point?"

"Difficult man," she snapped.

"I'm not, really. My mother always said I was a charming boy."

"She was clearly biased. Mothers always think their sons can do no wrong." Now sadness crossed her face, and he knew she was thinking of her son.

"Madeline." He reached a hand out to her.

"I'm fine. Look—" Suddenly she cried out, wrapping an arm across her stomach. Pain twisted her features.

He'd seen hints that she was in pain the night before, too, but he'd let her brush it off. Not this time.

"What's wrong?"

Her face had gone pale.

"That's it. I'm taking you to Medical."

"I'm fine. I'm not going to Medical."

"Madeline—"

"No." She shook her head, a wobble in her voice. "I don't want any more poking and prodding. They checked me over when I arrived and gave me a clean bill of health." She straightened. "I'm fine, just worried about Blaine." She pulled in a long breath. "I'll help you with your show." The words came out in a rush.

Lore felt a shot of satisfaction. "You might just

enjoy yourself."

"I doubt it," she said, bad-temperedly.

"I'll send an outfit to your room."

Her eyes widened. "Outfit?"

"It's all part of the show, Madeline. We have to set the scene. It's all part of getting the information we need from Vashto and Cerria."

She muttered under her breath. "Fine." She started to turn away.

He grabbed her arm. "You'll watch me fight tonight?"

"I'll be there. I'll be watching everyone."

He leaned in close, getting a hint of whatever scent she'd rubbed on her skin. It wasn't flowers, something deeper and muskier that once again made him believe that there was heat buried in Madeline Cochran.

"I think you're lying, *dushla*." This close to her, he sensed the rising warmth on her skin. It was a neat little skill common to the males of his species.

"You've called me that before. What's it mean?" She kept her tone brisk and he knew she was trying to change the subject.

"It means *little fire*." He tugged on her hair. "I think you'll be watching me. You like watching me."

Her blue eyes sparked. "You are so arrogant. And I should know—I've been dealing with arrogant men my entire life."

"My mother accused me of overconfidence as well."

"She knows you well."

Lore felt a slashing pain. "She did. Before she was killed."

Madeline fell silent. "I'm sorry."

"It's hard to lose those you love."

Her lips pressed together. "Do you have a child?"

"No."

"The pain of losing a child is unimaginable." She took a step back. "I'll see you tonight."

She turned to walk away, the subtle sway of her hips under her tunic and trousers drawing his gaze. She had delicious curves that she preferred to hide, rather than showcase.

Lore wanted to follow her. He wanted to pull her in close and hold her. Soothe her.

But just like that pet lizard he'd had, he knew that in this moment, she'd scratch and bite.

He needed more patience. He turned his gaze to a sky that was turning from pale blue to dark purple as the suns set. And more determination.

He smiled to himself. His mother had always accused him of being stubborn, too.

Chapter Three

Madeline sat in the stands, her hands twisted together in her lap. Her eyes were glued to the arena below. She was gobsmacked.

She'd attended a few arena fights in the last few weeks. She'd watched sword clash against sword, and blood splatter the sand.

But this spectacle wasn't like anything she'd ever seen before. All around her, the tiers of stone seats of the massive arena were packed with screaming spectators.

Down below, the arena floor had been transformed. It was filled with water, with flat-bottomed boats floating on them. The boats were made of a dark, black wood with sharp, reinforced prows for ramming other boats. A few had masts with white sails flapping in the wind. Expectant energy throbbed off the crowd.

They were waiting for the gladiators to appear.

"They use a mix of holographic technology and real-life objects to change the arena," Regan said from beside Madeline. The other woman was popping some sort of popcorn-like snack into her mouth.

"It's incredible." God, Jack would love this. Her

son was as obsessed by history as he was by space.

"The boats have hidden engines," Rory added from Madeline's other side. "I got to do some maintenance work on them. The sails are for show."

Somewhere, high above them, some of the crowd started to stomp their feet. Madeline saw movement on the other side of the arena.

The rival gladiators appeared. They swam out of a flooded tunnel, with powerful strokes of their arms.

"The House of Man'u," Galen said from behind Madeline. He was sitting quietly, his big body somehow relaxed, but at the same time, filled with tension. Madeline was pretty sure the imperator would leap into action in an instant if required. She wondered what he'd been like in the arena.

The gladiators climbed aboard the nearest boats and she turned her attention back to them. She saw the Man'u had very pale skin that had a rainbow-colored sheen to it, and ridges on their faces. But any prettiness from their skin was balanced out by the hard muscles beneath it and their silver-blue armor.

Now everyone was just waiting for the House of Galen gladiators to arrive.

She leaned back toward Galen. "Where are the couple you invited?"

Galen subtly moved his head. "Up in a private box I organized for them."

She glanced at the railings of the private boxes higher in the stands. The House of Galen seats were closest to the arena floor.

Then a hush fell over the crowd. People were turning around and looking up toward the top of the stands. Madeline twisted, Rory and Regan doing the same.

A single tall gladiator stood at the top of the arena. Even though his powerful body was covered in sleek, fish-scale armor that left his muscled abdomen bare and he wore a beaten-metal helmet, she knew instantly it was Lore. Something deep inside her just seemed attuned to him.

He raised one arm and whispers raced through the crowd.

He tossed something into the air.

Silver-and-red smoke exploded outward. The crowd screamed in delight, and the smoke twisted and turned. In it, Madeline caught glimpses of things: giant fish, sea serpents, alien sharks. The smoke shifted shape and took on the form of a giant, many-tentacled creature, like a kraken of myth. It launched itself over the arena, and then exploded outward before dissipating.

The crowd went wild.

In the next instant, the House of Galen gladiators strode out of a doorway at the top of the arena. They walked down the stairs with powerful strides, weapons in hand. Raiden and Harper led the way. Raiden's tattoos gleamed, his red cloak flaring behind him. Harper wore the same fish scale armor over her arms and was also wearing a red cloak that matched Raiden's. They looked magnificent.

Right behind them were Kace and Saff—the military-trained gladiator standing tall with his staff and the strong, elegant Saff smiling from beside him. Big Thorin and a new recruit that Madeline didn't recognize were next. And bringing up the rear were Nero and Lore.

They sure made an impact. Madeline couldn't help but stare, their strength and power radiating off them.

Of course, her gaze went to Lore. He'd rubbed oil over his skin where it showed between the sections of armor, and it gleamed under the arena lights.

As they walked past the House of Galen seats, big Thorin stopped and swept Regan into his arms for a deep kiss. The crowd cheered and whistled.

Rory waggled her fingers at Kace, one hand pressed to her belly. A small smile crossed the gladiator's face.

"Going to give me a kiss? For luck?"

Lore's sexy voice drawled in Madeline's ear, and she glanced up to see him right beside her seat. He looked even better up close. Most of his face was covered by the helmet, but his silver-gray eyes glinted through the eye slits. And his heavily-ridged stomach was right at her eye level. A trickle of traitorous heat curled in her belly. She couldn't remember the last time she'd been attracted to a man. *Damn hormones.*

"I don't think you need it," she told him.

He smiled. "But I'd sure enjoy it." He reached out and touched the shell of her ear. When he pulled his hand back, he was holding a shiny coin with the symbol of the House of Galen—a helmeted gladiator in profile—engraved on it. He handed it to her.

She took the coin, their fingers brushing. Then with a wink, he was gone.

When the gladiators reached the railing, they climbed up and dived into the water below. Heart hammering, the noise of the crowd in her ears, she watched them slice through the water toward their boats.

She watched as Lore strode across the deck of his boat, his sword in hand. Engines rumbled to life, a loud growl that echoed through the air.

A long, mournful siren rang out across the arena. The fight had begun.

The boats moved much faster than she'd anticipated. She watched Raiden and Harper's boat cut through the water and slam into the side of a House of Man'u boat. Seconds later, Raiden leaped across the gap between the boats and engaged the gladiators. Swords crashed against swords.

Madeline found her pulse tripping, and she leaned forward.

She watched Lore and Nero racing across the water, chasing a Man'u boat. Then, a hidden Man'u gladiator appeared from out of the water, climbing stealthily aboard Lore's craft. The opponent hefted a giant axe.

God. Her fingers tightened on the coin. *Lore, turn around.*

The gladiator crept forward, but at the last second, Lore turned and struck with his sword.

Blood bloomed on the Man'u gladiator's shoulder, and then he and Lore were locked in a vicious fight.

She watched as Lore forced the other gladiator back. There was no ease or charm on Lore's face now—it was all hard-set lines of concentration.

The Man'u gladiator hit the side of the boat and teetered there. Lore lifted a boot, planted it in the man's gut, and tipped him overboard. He landed in the water with a splash.

Yes. Madeline raised her voice to cheer with the crowd.

"Addictive, isn't it?"

She glanced at Rory and gave a small nod. Beside her, Regan's face was flushed with excitement, her gaze glued to Thorin, who was currently roaring fiercely, and using his axe to chop down the mast of a Man'u boat.

Madeline turned back, her belly alive with flutters that had nothing to do with anxiety or food disagreeing with her. She watched Lore climb up the mast on his boat with a powerful flex of arms and legs. He paused at the top, waving to the crowd, before he touched his belt. A moment later, he threw something into the air.

Fireworks rocketed upward, and burst high above the crowd in a shower of brilliant colors.

As Nero steered the boat, it came close to another of the opponent's boats. She watched as Lore grabbed a rope tied to the mast. He pushed off and swung across the gap from one boat to the other. The crowd gasped, and so did Madeline.

He landed on the deck of the other boat in a

crouch, and then he was up, attacking the nearest Man'u.

Madeline swallowed, excitement flooding her. Lore looked like a dashing pirate. She watched him fight, knocking one gladiator into the water and slashing another one across the chest. For all his charm and showiness, he was a hell of a fighter. It was easy to forget that his lean muscles were honed to precision by all of the fighting, and that he was seriously experienced with his sword.

The minutes raced by, boats cutting across the water, sword striking sword. Lore jerked back suddenly, a line of red appearing on his belly, and she winced, her mouth going dry. But the cut didn't appear to slow him down. *He's done this a thousand times, Madeline.*

Then the crowd erupted with shouts and cries, and she blinked. *It was over already?* She scanned the boats. All of the House of Man'u gladiators were down and defeated.

The House of Galen gladiators all swung across to one boat, and, standing together, raised their fists into the air. The cheering from their fans was deafening.

As the announcers declared the House of Galen the winners, the crowd made even more noise. Madeline smiled. And then she gave a small start. She couldn't remember the last time she smiled, or even felt this much excitement coursing through her.

Right at this moment, she wasn't thinking about herself or her problems.

Suddenly, she saw Lore grab another rope again. He pushed off from the boat, swinging directly toward the House of Galen seats.

Her heart knocked against her chest. He landed on the railing right in front of her.

Regan jumped up and pecked his cheek. "Nice fight."

Rory leaned over and smacked a hand against his flank. "Good one, Lore."

But Lore was staring at Madeline. With one hand still holding the rope, he used the other to yank off his helmet. His tawny hair was damp and his eyes were glittering.

He didn't say a word, but she heard his silent dare louder than if he'd shouted it at her.

She told herself to stay seated, but instead, she stood and took a step toward him.

He used his free arm to sweep her against his chest. He smelled of heat, sweat and blood, and when he bent her over his arm, like some romance hero, excitement flared.

Around them, the crowd's cheers echoed off the ancient stone of the arena. Then he leaned down and pressed his mouth to hers, and there was only Lore.

His tongue swept into her mouth, hot and hungry. Madeline felt like she'd been hit by an electric shock or a tsunami. She moaned and kissed him back.

But his mouth took complete and utter ownership of hers. He kissed with an untamed power that rocked her, like she was being consumed.

Heat flooded her. It was so hot and shocking, so much feeling coursing through her. She hadn't realized her life had been so cold and lacking, until she felt the heat of Lore wrap around her.

He pulled back, and all she could do was look up at him, stunned. She felt the blood he'd smeared on her clothes and knew that should horrify her, but it didn't.

He touched her cheek, that single touch searing, then he smiled and let her go. Before her brain cells even started firing again, he'd gripped the rope and swung back to his friends.

***

Madeline couldn't believe she'd agreed to this stupid idea. Or this stupid dress.

She hurried out of her room and through the corridors. It would take her a few minutes to get from the House of Galen back up to the rooms where the after party was being held.

After the sea battle had ended, the gladiators had all headed out to bathe and change. Her lips still burning from that kiss, Madeline had made her way straight to the party room to lose herself in some work. She'd helped hang decorations, triple-checked everything was okay with the food and drinks, and checked in with the dancers she'd hired from the District with the help of Galen's very efficient staff. His people had been suspicious of her at first, but now, she had a good working relationship going with them.

Everything was perfect for the party, and the guests would be arriving soon.

She'd squeezed out a few minutes for herself to shower and change. When she'd arrived back at her room, her outfit from Lore had arrived and been laid out on her bed. She sniffed. She wasn't thinking about this sorry excuse for a dress she had on. Right now, she needed to focus on the party. She needed everything to go off without a hitch. Blaine's life depended on it.

Her stomach gave an uncomfortable grind and she grimaced. Anxiety. That was all. She'd never thought she'd miss antacids.

She strode into the party room. Walls of glass gave a perfect view of the arena below which was still filled with water, the now-empty boats resting on the glassy surface. The night sky was filled with stars, and since the moon had yet to rise, she could just make out a faint, pink-hued nebula to the east.

Turning, she focused on the room. She'd gone for a water theme in honor of the mock sea battle. Ribbons of silvery-blue fell from the ceiling, and elegant, twisted, blue glass art pieces were dotted around the room. They almost looked like ice, and each time she looked at them, she saw different shapes: slender women, elegant spinning dancers, entwined lovers. Across the room, the servers were setting out food on long tables.

The *pièce de résistance* was on the back wall. A large tank of water was filled with long-haired women who were dancing through the water like mermaids, their hair flowing out behind them. Their long, sinuous bodies were covered in tiny, glittery outfits. The women were water dancers she'd borrowed from the Dark Nebula Casino. They were an alien species who could breathe under water. Madeline had to admit, they looked pretty impressive.

A sharp, appreciative whistle cut through the room, and she turned. Harper, Regan, and Rory were striding toward her.

"The place looks *amazing*." Rory's gaze skated down Madeline. "And so do you, Mads."

Madeline ran a hand down the dress. "Uh, Lore demanded I wear it." The slip of fabric looked like liquid water. It caught the light, reflecting it back and was the same blue as her eyes. It clung to every curve and had two high slits that left her feeling bare, but at least it felt incredibly soft when she moved.

"Lore, huh?" Rory shot her a wide grin.

Madeline's stomach started up that all-too-familiar churn. "It's not like that. I know all of you have lost your heads over alien gladiators, but not me. This isn't my life."

"There's no way home, Madeline," Regan said quietly. "This *is* our life, now."

"There's no way back to Earth that we know of *yet*. I'm not ready to give up." She couldn't give up on Jack.

Harper was watching Madeline's face intently. "There's good here, Madeline, if you look for it."

Madeline's throat tightened, and she didn't respond.

"Lore's a good man and he's a good fighter under all the flair," Harper continued.

Rory gave a decisive nod. "And the man is mighty fine to look at."

"And he's nice," Regan added.

"The last thing I need right now is a male of any description," Madeline told them. "The ones I've known in the past have always proven untrustworthy. Except for my son."

Regan's face turned sad. "I'm sorry. You must miss him."

"I haven't given up on seeing him again one day."

"Madeline—" Rory began.

Madeline held up her hand. "Don't worry. I'm being realistic about our circumstances, but I will exhaust every option first." She set her shoulders back, the low-grade throb in her stomach making her wish for an antacid. "For now, we have a party to put on in order to find Blaine."

Behind them, voices echoed as guests started entering the room. *Showtime.*

Chapter Four

Madeline was too busy to think of anything except the party. She checked in on the chefs, the bartenders, and the entertainers. The burning in her stomach was growing, but she didn't have the time or desire to eat. The place was packed with guests mingling, talking, and laughing. Many had gathered around the water dancers, enjoying the show.

Then the gladiators arrived.

Instantly, the room felt more crowded. Most of the gladiators towered over everyone else in the room. Some of them had showered and changed, but some of them hadn't. Galen had told her many of the fans enjoyed seeing the gladiators sweat-slicked and blood-splattered. As Madeline scanned the room, she could see that several of the guests loved it.

Raiden, Thorin, and Kace instantly moved toward their women, ignoring anyone trying to gain their attention. Madeline watched for a second, as Thorin swept a smiling Regan off her feet. She looked tiny compared to her alien gladiator. Raiden tugged Harper to his side and she rested her head against his chest. Kace leaned over Rory, pressing a sweet kiss to her lips.

Something inside Madeline clenched hard. She didn't want that, so why did it make her feel so damn jealous?

Against her will, her gaze swept the entrance, seeking a tawny-haired gladiator.

There was no sign of Lore. Turning, Madeline busied herself checking the food service, and ensuring the hors d'oeuvres were making it out among the guests.

"I just got our guests of honor settled."

Galen stepped up beside her. A dark look was on his face, and he nodded his head toward the side of the room where round couches had been set up.

Her gaze zeroed in on the couple lounging on a blue couch and the burning in her stomach increased. There was only one word to describe the pair…scary.

The man was rough-looking, with a heavy jaw, dark eyes, and scars crossing his face. Although he was seated, she knew he'd tower over almost everyone in the room—gladiators included. The woman beside him was tall and slender. She had her long, leather-encased legs crossed, and was stroking the back of a near-naked male sitting at her feet. As the woman sipped a drink, Madeline got a good view of the woman's sharp face. Her cheekbones looked like blades, and her almond-shaped eyes were a glittering gold. She smiled and Madeline hissed in a breath. The woman had a mouthful of pointed, sharp teeth.

"Cerria loves men," Galen said. "Word is Vashto indulges her and likes to watch."

"I don't really care what they like, I only care what they know."

Galen gave a single nod. "Just be careful."

In the next instant, Lore entered, looking around the room with a smile. He'd showered, and was dressed in a black shirt and black leather pants. He looked delicious, and still an awful lot like a pirate.

Instantly, three curvaceous arena flutterers converged on him, and Madeline felt her throat tighten.

"Madeline?"

As one of the kitchen staff grabbed her attention, Madeline forced her gaze away from Lore and his admirers. She followed the woman into the kitchen to deal with a problem over some live bug dish that was being served. Madeline averted her gaze from the slimy, black, slug-like creatures, her stomach turning over. Apparently, these things were a delicacy. With the problem finally solved, she headed back into the party.

Drinks were flowing. People were laughing. Vashto and Cerria were watching the water dancers with interest. Everything was running smoothly.

Madeline felt someone come up behind her, warm breath puffing on the back of her neck.

"Where have you been hiding?" Lore drawled.

She spun to face him. This close to him, she

smelled the scent of his freshly washed skin. "Taking care of some things."

"Organizing things and working too hard." His gaze moved to the giant aquarium filled with the dancers. "You've done an amazing job, Madeline."

"It's all to get our special guests to open up." She eyed the couple. Cerria was sitting in the lap of a naked male, laughing uproariously. "If we get something that we can use to find Blaine, it'll all be worth it." She turned back to see him looking at her dress.

He fingered the tiny strap that tied up behind her neck. "I knew this Bollian silk would look fabulous on you."

She arched a brow. "Perhaps you should have bought a whole dress, not half of one."

That charming grin. "You have lovely shoulders and legs. I enjoy looking at them."

She huffed out a breath. The man was incorrigible.

He touched her hair, sifting some of the strands through his fingers. The look on his face made her heart clench.

"You're incredibly beautiful, Madeline. With or without the silk."

No one had ever called her beautiful. Smart, sharp, cunning, bitch...she'd heard all of those before. But no man had ever looked at her with such curiosity or desire—like she was something precious for him to uncover.

"Thank you." She cleared her throat. "Are you ready to start your show?"

"Are you ready to be my assistant?"

"Not really, but let's get this over and done with."

He took her hand and led her over to the small stage that had been set up near the windows.

Madeline moved up to the tiny microphone device the staff had brought in. "Ladies and gentlemen, I'd like to welcome you to the House of Galen."

Cheers erupted.

"I hope you're enjoying our celebration."

More cheers and lifted drinks.

"Now we have something extra special for you." The lights lowered, leaving the guests in dim light. "Our own showman gladiator is going to put on a very special show. One you can't see anywhere else. One that will wow you and leave you a little breathless."

Murmurs rippled through the guests. Madeline saw Cerria pressed into Vashto's side, watching the stage with acute interest.

"Please welcome Lore, son of Uma, grandson of Xilene."

She stepped backward as Lore strode forward. A single beam of white-blue light illuminated him. He stood tall and straight, looking both mysterious and approachable.

He threw his arm up, then turned one palm skyward. For a second, nothing happened, then the spectators closest to the makeshift stage gasped.

A tiny bubble of water appeared on his palm.

Madeline stared. It looked like a tiny crystal or

diamond. He lifted his other hand over it, until the small bubble of water was pressed between his palms. Then he started moving his hands apart, like he was working taffy, pulling the ball bigger and bigger.

The crowd, and Madeline, watched, mesmerized, as the ball of water increased in size. Soon it was over a meter wide.

"If my lovely assistant would please bring me that small box behind her."

Madeline grabbed the glimmering metallic box and moved up beside him. The spotlight was far brighter than she'd imagined and she fought not to blink.

"Open it."

She flicked open the lid. Inside was a tiny, polished, multicolored rock. She frowned. What was he going to do with that?

He pulled out the tiny rock and tossed it into the bubble of water. She watched the rock sink slowly, then a second later, it burst open, turning into a brightly colored fish.

Madeline's delighted gasp matched the crowd's. As the small creature swam around the ball, the guests applauded.

"Now, let's make this more exciting." Lore snapped his fingers and the fish disappeared. He gripped the water orb on either side and again worked it until it grew even larger. The giant blue sphere floated in front of him until it was as tall as he was.

"And now, I need my lovely assistant's help." He

held out a hand to her.

Madeline set her hand into his.

"Your turn," he told her.

"What?"

"Trust me," he murmured.

She didn't trust anybody, but strangely enough, with his big, warm hand holding hers, she let him help her step *inside* the ball of water.

Madeline expected it to actually be an entire ball of water, but instead it was only a giant bubble. She could breathe just fine and float around. She held her arms out, feeling like she was as light as a feather.

Lore raised his hands up and the orb of water lifted off the ground. Madeline's heart leaped in her throat. *Trust him. He won't hurt you.*

She looked down and saw the crowd looking up at her in awe. She was grateful the fabric of her dress clung to her legs and didn't give them a view of her underwear. A giddy laugh caught in her throat. She glanced at Lore and saw he was motioning for her to spin around.

What the hell? Recalling skills from her days as a high-school gymnast, Madeline turned in a somersault, a laugh escaping her throat. She kicked and floated back upright.

Below, Lore leaped up onto a table until he could reach her bubble. He touched the sides again, enlarging it more.

Then he climbed inside with her.

"This is incredible," she said breathlessly.

"I thought you might like it." He held her hand,

and, with his other hand, he waved forward. The ball of water moved out over the party guests. They were all reaching up, women laughing, men looking on wide-eyed.

Lore moved the bubble around the room. Inside it, they spun around together and Madeline turned a few more somersaults with his help. Soon, the orb was floating back over the stage.

"Ready for the finale?" he asked.

Madeline wasn't sure she was ready for anything, where this man was concerned. But she nodded anyway.

He wrapped his arms around her and pulled her close. Then he kissed her.

His taste exploded in her mouth, and at the same moment, the water disappeared. Madeline felt herself drop, and a startled scream lodged in her throat.

The next thing she knew, she was held tight in Lore's arms as he landed on the stage, flexing his knees slightly at the impact. Madeline clutched at his shoulders, watching as the water splashed across the floor around them.

Then Lore lifted a hand and waved it in a wide arc. The water ignited, bursting into a ring of flames around them.

The crowd went wild, applause filling the room. The spotlight flicked off, leaving Lore and Madeline in firelight.

"That was amazing. How do you do it?" she asked. "The water? The fire?"

She saw his smile in the dim light. "Don't you

believe in magic?"

"No. Magic doesn't exist."

"Well, then you should know that a showman never gives his secrets away."

He set her on her feet and snapped his fingers. The flames shut off in an instant. Then he grabbed her hand and pulled her off the stage. He tugged her around a large support pillar, giving them the illusion of privacy.

"You must practice all these illusions a lot." She frowned to herself. Surely something this elaborate would have required him to set things up beforehand? But she knew for a fact he hadn't been up here earlier.

He held his palm up. A small flame flickered to life in the center of it.

Madeline gripped his thick wrist, studying all around. She just couldn't see how he could do it. She reached out and flicked her finger through the flame.

It was hot.

Lore leaned down and blew out the flame. Then he lifted his hands and ran them up her bare arms. She felt the warmth radiating off his skin. She stared hard at his strong forearms and gasped. The veins in his arms were glowing a warm gold color.

"You can't always trust what you see." He reached out and tapped his finger over her heart, just above her breast. "You have to trust what you feel."

Madeline wasn't sure she could trust anything right now. Especially not with his warm touch sending parts of her that had nothing to do with magic and illusion up in flames. And she knew she really couldn't trust how she felt, because all the emotions inside her lately were just a big, painful jumble of confusion.

Suddenly Galen's stocky silhouette appeared. "Looks like you did too good of a job."

Lore's hands tightened on Madeline. "Why?"

"Vashto and Cerria want to meet you both." The imperator's face was serious. "Tread carefully, but make it good."

Chapter Five

As Lore walked across the crowded room, he instantly spotted the couple lounging on a blue couch. His muscles tensed.

He didn't like the look of them. The man was big, tough, and scarred. He had faint patches of a scale-like pattern on his skin, so he had some reptilian heritage. The woman sat on the seat back, her legs tucked in close beside Vashto. He was idly stroking them, his fingers disappearing occasionally under her clothing.

The woman was all sharp angles, with slanted eyes and high cheekbones. Her skin was a deep amber color. Her gaze locked with Lore's and she lifted a hand to tap her nails against her plump lips. Her hands were tipped with long claws. She licked her lips.

Vashto's gaze landed on Madeline, hot, hungry and predatory. Lore pulled her closer to his side.

"Welcome." Cerria's voice was a deep, raspy purr. She waved a hand at the couch beside her. "Please join us. We enjoyed your show immensely."

Lore sat down, careful to put himself between Madeline and the couple. Cerria reached out and scraped her claws down Lore's arm.

"I also enjoyed your battle in the arena. You fought well, gladiator." A nictitating membrane flicked over her eyes. "We won money on you. A lot of money."

Vashto leaned forward. "And your show here this evening was...entertaining." The man's voice was a deep rumble. His eyes ran down Madeline's bare legs and his tongue flicked out to lick his lips. It was thin and forked.

Lore reached over and pressed his palm against Madeline's thigh. She was as tense as a new recruit in the arena. "I'm glad you enjoyed it. Madeline and I work very well together."

"We like shows and fights and delicious things." Cerria bared her teeth and reached out to touch Lore's chest.

Madeline's hand shot out and grabbed the woman's wrist.

Cerria pulled back with a narrowed gaze. Madeline pressed her palm over Lore's beating heart. He liked the feel of her touch as much as he liked seeing her stake a claim.

Lore cleared his throat, knowing that they had to walk a delicate line of keeping Cerria happy and not letting her sink her sharp teeth into them. "I've always been interested in fighting...and gambling. Both are fascinating games and tests of skill."

Cerria leaned forward, seemingly diverted. "Exactly! Fun and challenging."

Lore inclined his head. "It's part of the reason why I ended up here in the arena." He shrugged. "But sometimes—" he glanced around, lowering his voice "—I don't find the fights that exciting anymore. They feel too...staged." He scowled. "And I don't get time to bet on any good fights anymore."

Cerria's face lit up. "We can hook you up."

Lore stilled. "Really?" He glanced at Vashto and the man nodded.

"If you want to fight, really fight, we can suggest your name. And as for betting—" Cerria scraped a nail down Vashto's neck "—we can get you in to bet on the bloodiest, goriest fights in Kor Magna."

"I might be interested in that." Lore made another show of looking around and lowering his voice. "It has to be between us. Galen can't find out."

Vashto's brows pulled together. "No, I can imagine you wouldn't want to cross a man like Galen."

"He can be...brutal," Lore said.

"Really?" Cerria's voice turned considering, her gaze scanning the room for the imperator. Then she leaned forward, crossing her long legs and licking her lips. "These are secret fights. *Really* good secret fights. They aren't pretty or flashy." She poked out her tongue and ran a claw down it, until a line of red blood appeared. "Lots and lots of yummy red blood."

Lore pretended to look interested. The woman clearly got off on other people's pain. "They're fights to the death?"

"Yes." Cerria's voice was breathless.

Vashto nodded. "Still keen?"

Lore nodded. "Let me know."

"There's going to be a big fight in a few days," the man said. "It's hidden."

"How do I get an invite?"

"Tomorrow night there's a party," Vashto said. "People attend, have fun, enjoy the pleasures on offer…and some people will receive invites to the fight."

"I love a party." Cerria clapped her hands together. "Come! Come!"

Lore nodded. "I'd love to." He felt Madeline stiffen beside him.

"And how about right now?" Cerria drew her claws down Lore's cheek. "How about a private party, gladiator? My man likes to watch me being a bad girl."

Lore tasted bile in his mouth. "Tempting."

Madeline shifted closer. "But no."

Cerria's nose wrinkled. "She can come too, if you want."

Lore stood and gave Cerria a courtly bow. "Like I said, tempting, but we have other plans this evening." He pulled Madeline up from the couch. "I hope you enjoy the rest of the party." He looked at Vashto. "I'll wait to hear from you."

As fast as he could, Lore led Madeline away. As soon as they were swallowed by the crowd, he stopped and grabbed a drink. Madeline did the same, gulping the liquid down.

She wrinkled her nose. "I feel dirty."

He nodded. "You aren't alone."

"But it's a good lead, isn't it?"

"It is. If I can attend this party and get an invite

to the fights, there's a good chance I'll find Blaine." He reached out and touched her hair, pushing it back behind her ear. For some strange reason, Lore loved her ears—they were perfectly formed. "You did well. And you defended me."

She stiffened. "You're helping me, so I thought I should return the favor."

"It wasn't necessary."

Now she went even stiffer. "You...you *wanted* to go with her?"

"Hardly—"

"Whatever." Madeline waved a hand. "I need to—"

He grabbed her shoulders and pulled her close, lowering his voice. "I like some sharp edges, but only when they're hiding soft and sexy beneath them." He rubbed his fingers over her soft skin. "I don't like a woman who gets off on someone else's pain."

Madeline trembled, then tried to pull away. "I have to check on the servers."

"You're always finding something to keep you busy," he said. "Don't you ever just do something pleasurable? For yourself. Or better yet, do nothing."

She looked like he'd asked if she liked to dance naked in space. "No."

"You should try it."

"I like to be busy." She took another large gulp of her drink. "It keeps me—"

"From thinking?" He understood. When he'd first been sold to the arena, he'd done the same.

Except he'd filled the hours with fighting and fucking.

A spasm crossed her face. "Yes."

Then Lore watched as every drop of color leached out of her cheeks. He frowned. "Madeline—"

She let out a small cry, and her glass dropped from her hand, shattering on the floor. Because of the crowd and the loud music, no one even glanced their way. She wrapped her arms around her middle and made a pained noise.

"Hold on." He picked her up into his arms.

"I'm fine."

"You're not fine." He pushed through the crowd, ignoring Raiden and Thorin, who were subtly trying to get his attention. "You've gone as white as the Naskian salt plains." He found a couch in a dark corner of the room. A Gallian man was sitting on it, but as Lore glared at him, the poor guest shot to his feet and scurried away.

He set her down, kneeling beside her. Her color was still not great. "I'm taking you to Medical."

"No! I promise I'm fine." She ran a shaky hand through her hair. "I'm okay. I haven't eaten, that's all."

He stared at her, seeing that some color was slowly seeping back into her cheeks. "You need to look after yourself better than this, Madeline."

She nodded. "I was just nervous about this evening. I'll make sure I eat something, and as soon as this party is over, I'm heading straight to bed."

Lore still wasn't convinced. Too many times now he'd seen that look of pain cross her face.

"Thanks for your help tonight," she said quietly. "The show, talking with Vashto and Cerria. Without you, we wouldn't be on the right path to finding Blaine." She plucked at the hem of her dress.

"I'll do everything I can to help him." *And to help you. If you'll let me.*

She nodded, looking over his shoulder. "I see Harper and Rory." She stood. "Thanks again, Lore."

She brushed past him, and Lore fought the urge to follow her.

But he let her go for now. Pushing her too hard wouldn't help. He got the feeling no one had ever taken care of Madeline before. He couldn't stop the urge to take care of her, it was built into his very being. He wanted to see her happy and healthy, and…he really wanted her naked beneath him.

Whether she liked it or not, Madeline Cochran was going to be his.

***

Madeline woke with a gasp. She was in agony.

She pressed her hands against her burning stomach, rolling to the edge of her bed. The pain was outrageous.

Milk. She wanted some of the milky drink she'd found earlier in the kitchen. It had helped ease her stomach after the party.

Her room was awash in moonlight, and she

stumbled through the shadows, clad only in her sleep shirt. It was a little too big and kept slipping off one shoulder, but at least it fell almost to her knees.

She staggered down the hallway, hoping she wouldn't run into anybody. But it was late, the party having ended hours ago. Everyone should be sleeping by now.

She moved into the living area reserved for the high-level gladiators. A small kitchen area in the corner was kept well-stocked by the main kitchen staff. After rummaging through the cupboards, she found a glass and filled it with the milky liquid.

Madeline took a sip and tried not to wonder what alien animal it had come from. She waited for the drink to have some effect, but this time, it didn't help. The horrible burning felt like acid gnawing a hole in her insides.

Stumbling away from the kitchen, she moved back through the dark living space. When a sharp spear of agony rocketed through her, she slammed into the wall. God, it hurt.

She headed toward the balcony. Maybe some fresh air would help? But she only made it to the window before another sharp pain cut through her. Pressing her forehead to the cool glass, she felt the prick of tears. She was miserable. Alone. And she missed her son more than anything.

She stared out the window at the shadowed city beyond. An alien city so far from everything that was familiar to her. Here, she was nothing. Here, she felt like the glass she was looking through—

transparent and insubstantial.

All of a sudden, a light clicked on. "Madeline?"

Not now. She lifted her head. A bare-chested Lore, clad only in some soft-looking gray trousers, stood in the doorway to the living area. He always saw her at her weakest.

"Go back to bed," she said.

"What's wrong?" He moved closer, his brow knitted.

"Everything." The word rushed out of her. "I've lost everything."

He stopped beside her. "I've noticed you haven't cried since that day you first arrived."

She felt the heat pouring off him, and she couldn't meet his gaze. "What would a big, bad gladiator know about women and crying?"

"I grew up in a family of women. I was raised by my grandmother and my mother, and surrounded by my aunts and cousins."

She looked up now. "All women?"

He nodded. "My species, the Nomi, don't give birth to male children very often. Mostly, the women mate with males of other species, but come back to raise their children in our matriarchal family units."

"Like the Amazon," Madeline murmured.

"Nomi genes are dominant, so the children are always Nomi, and most often, female. So, believe me, I know all about a woman's tears, in all their many forms."

Madeline pressed her arm against the window to hold herself upright. "Tears are for the weak. They don't help anything."

He edged closer, his crisp, male scent wrapping around her.

"Tears help you purge the pain," he said quietly.

She made a scoffing sound. "You're telling me that you cry?"

"I did when pirates attacked my family's spaceship. The Nomi are nomads, and we live in space, usually traveling in convoy. My grandmother, Xilene, owned our ship and ran our convoy. She was a tough, old woman and a fierce captain. My mother and aunts were the crew."

Madeline heard the fondness buried in his words. "What happened?"

"We were overrun by pirate slavers. I was young and not much of a fighter." Something painful crossed his face. "My grandmother and mother were killed in front of me." His gaze turned a stormy gray. "My sister and I were taken as slaves. I was sold here to the arena."

He'd been abducted, too, and lost his family. Just like her. Madeline pressed her hand to her churning belly, rubbing it in a circle, as she took in his strong, steady form. "You…never found your sister?"

"After I earned my freedom, I looked for her." He drew in a deep breath. "The trail had gone cold years ago, but I spent several years and all my earnings looking until there was nowhere else to look. It's hard not knowing."

"Yes." She looked at him, her gaze falling on his warm, tanned throat. He'd lost it all, but had found a way to survive. To build a new life.

"It's okay to lean a little," he told her.

"I don't lean. I—" She gave another strangled cry as agony spiked.

Something scary flashed on his face this time. "*Drak*. What are you doing to yourself?"

He came closer and she held her hands up. "Don't touch me."

He ignored her. Seconds later, she found herself scooped up and settled on the surface of the nearby dining table.

Lore studied her face. "Relax. Breathe."

She tried, but every breath hurt. "Just leave me alone."

"How often has this been happening?" he demanded. "More than the few times I've seen you in pain?"

"It's just stress."

"Quit being stubborn. I just want to help you." He reached out, his hand tangling in her hair.

Madeline felt her eyelashes flutter. A part of her wanted to lean. Just for a little while. Until everything stopped hurting.

But in her life, good things only ever came when she fought for them herself. The few times she'd risked leaning on somebody else, they always disappeared and left her falling.

"I'm fine." She slid off the table to prove her point, gritting her teeth hard. "Please don't mention this to Harper and the others."

She had to get away from him. Moving as fast as she could, she crossed the room. As she reached the corridor leading to the bedrooms, another attack hit. The pain caused sweat to break out on her skin.

She slammed open the door to her bedroom, and took two steps inside. Another fierce wave of pain hit, and drove her to the floor. She stayed there on her hands and knees, fire roaring through her belly.

"Luckily, I'm as stubborn as you." Lore's arms wrapped around her, strong and secure.

Madeline groaned and coughed. Blood splattered onto the floor.

The world shifted as she was spun and lifted up into Lore's arms. His face was the fiercest she'd seen it, even in the arena. He pressed her into his hard chest.

"No more excuses," he growled. "Medical. Now."

Chapter Six

Lore was mad and he didn't get mad often.

He held Madeline tight in his arms. He was feeling protective, and he didn't care who knew about it. She looked grumpy, rumpled, and in pain.

He'd never found any of that attractive before, but he felt a powerful pull toward her. He turned a corner and the doors to Medical were just ahead. He'd spent plenty of time in there before, being patched up after fights. Galen spent a lot of money on high-tech medical equipment, and the best healers in the galaxy.

He pushed open the doors with a hip. Inside, the space was clean and tidy. Lore had always thought the arena was the best illusion of all—ancient stone, sand, low tech. But in here was about as opposite as you could get.

Three regen tanks filled with blue liquid lined the back wall. Several narrow beds were lined up in a precise row, and other bits of high-tech medical equipment dotted the room.

One of the Hermia healers stepped forward, sand-colored robes whispering around the healer's long, slender body. The healer had a neutral face, that was calm and composed. He'd never seen a Hermia panic before. The healers were a genderless species with the ability to manipulate biological energies.

"She's getting a sharp pain in her stomach. She keeps saying she's fine but she's not."

The Hermia healer gestured to the closest bunk. "Please set her down here."

Lore did, but stayed close. The healer lifted a small, hand-held scanner.

Madeline stirred. "I really am fine. You, or one of your team, checked me out when I arrived here. There's no need—"

Lore sent her a look and her words cut off, her lips pressing together. The Hermia gently ran the scanner over Madeline's body. When the Hermia frowned, Lore felt his heart kick in his chest.

Usually, the healers barely showed any reaction, and they'd seen some pretty gory injuries after arena fights.

The Hermia lowered the scanner. "You have internal damage from the drugs that were used on you during your captivity."

Madeline gasped, and Lore grabbed her hand. He expected her to jerk away, but instead, she tangled her fingers with his and squeezed.

"I was given a clean bill of health when I came to the House of Galen," she said.

"Why didn't you find it before?" Lore demanded.

"This type of damage develops over time." The Hermia looked at them calmly. "It's exacerbated by stress and poor diet."

Lore scowled down at her and watched as she squirmed.

"I'm stuck here," she snapped. "Everything I love is gone and out of reach. The stress isn't going away anytime soon."

"You need to take better care of yourself," Lore said.

The Hermia nodded. "The gladiator is correct."

"If she won't do it, I'll help her with it," Lore said.

Blue eyes flashed up at him. "I don't need a keeper."

He felt a stab of anger and pressed his nose against hers. "Apparently, you do." He turned to look at the healer. "What does she need? You can treat this, right?"

The Hermia nodded, already holding a clear cup full of amber fluid. "Drink this. It will stop the pain and help the healing. But a lot of this damage can only be reversed by time." The Hermia's calm gaze landed on Lore. "She needs fresh food. Broths are good for healing her stomach. I recommend light exercise to help with her stress."

Madeline looked mutinous, but she took the cup and tossed back the medicine. Lore scooped her into his arms again.

"I can walk—"

"Shut it." He pulled her closer, nodded to the healer, and stormed out. Soon, he was setting her back on her bed. "Stay there, I'm going to make you some tea."

"I don't like tea."

"You'll like this one."

Ignoring her scowl, he quickly made his way to the kitchen. He pulled open cupboards until he found what he wanted. As the tea steeped, he closed his eyes for a second. Drak, she was stubborn. No wonder she hadn't let anyone close...her outer shell was made of finely-honed tarden metal—the toughest metal found in the occupied worlds.

Well, whether she liked it or not, she had a protector. He lifted the mug and headed back to her room.

She was sitting on the bed, looking unhappy. "Lore—"

He ignored her, sitting beside her and handing her the mug. She took it, eyeing it like it might explode in her face.

"This was my sister's favorite drink," he told her.

Leaning back against the pillows, Madeline took a sip. Her eyebrows rose. "It's pretty good. What's it called?"

"It's called Ar'bor. The tea leaves are harvested from a planet called Boreal, but I used to call it Yelena's drink."

"Was that her name?"

"Yes."

"What was she like?"

The now-faded picture of his sister filled his mind. He smiled. "Yelena was a firecracker. Always smiling, always moving, always busy."

"Do you...wonder where she is?"

"Every day."

"How do you cope?" Madeline stared down into the tea.

Lore knew she was thinking of her son. "You remember the good times. I remember Yelena's smile. The way she loved to dance. And I live, just in case she didn't get the chance."

Madeline's lips trembled. "My son, Jack, was born with a bad heart."

Her face was the softest Lore had ever seen it. "You worry about him."

She nodded. "He needed a transplant. His heart was failing when he was eight and the wait-list for donor hearts was long. Top-of-the-line, artificial hearts were available for purchase, but they were very, very expensive."

"You got it for him."

She nodded. "He's my child. I'd do anything for him." She took a deep breath. "I had a job as a food server and I didn't make a lot of money. Nor did Jack's father. We had Jack when we were both young, and separated when he was two. We were providing for him, but we weren't wealthy by any means."

Lore waited, watching the interesting emotions flitter across her face.

"So, I went back to school to complete an accelerated business course. Jack's father cared for him while I studied and worked hard. I knew jobs in space paid very well and I fought my way through getting a job at a space station corporation, fought for promotions, and finally got a job managing a space station. I was away from Jack, but I achieved the company objectives, no matter what, and my company loaned me the money to pay for Jack's heart. I just recently finished paying off that debt."

"You got him that heart, but you had to give up being with him."

She bit her lip and nodded. "I had to be in space to make the money. His father loves him, and Jack lives with him. I send...sent...most of my money back so they could have a good home."

She'd sacrificed so much for her son. "And now you worry how they'll go on without you."

She nodded. "I have a good trust fund set up for Jack, but..."

"He knows you love him, Madeline."

"I was gone for so long. And now, I'm gone for good."

Lore grabbed her slim shoulder and squeezed. "He knows, Madeline."

"I hope so."

"Rest now." He took the now-empty mug from her. He didn't mention that he'd also laced it with a sedative.

She turned her face into her pillow, her eyelids drooping. "So tired."

"Sleep." She looked delicate, almost vulnerable.

He shifted to set the cup down and her hand shot out, fingers curling around his arm.

"Please...don't leave me."

His chest tightened. "I won't."

With that, she finally relaxed and drifted into sleep. Lore sat there, content to watch her and the gentle rise and fall of her chest. He glanced at her bedside table and his muscles locked. The coin he'd given her sat there, beside a glass of water holding the white perra blossom he'd gifted her.

Sometimes the hardest shells hid the softest hearts. He remembered his grandmother teaching him that. She'd also taught him that the most important things were worth the wait.

***

Madeline stepped onto the sand of the training arena, the morning sunlight bright in her eyes. The large suns of Carthago looked like they were racing each other higher in the pale-blue sky.

"I don't have time for this," she muttered. "I have inventory to go over in the kitchen. I'm optimizing the system so Galen doesn't keep quite so many goods in storage. He's losing a portion of them when they go bad before they get used—"

"The healer said you had to exercise." Lore strode beside her, bare chest crisscrossed by leather straps, his voice radiating alpha-male stubbornness.

Oh, the man could toss out a smile and dispense the charm, but it was all a show. All of it hiding the bossy, obstinate man underneath.

Madeline had to admit that after a good night's sleep and whatever the healer had given her—not to mention the breakfast of fresh fruit and eggs that Lore had forced her to eat this morning—her stomach felt much better. She had more energy than she'd had in a long time.

She turned her attention to the training arena. It was far smaller than the main Kor Magna Arena, and solely for the House of Galen's use. Some new recruits were sparring on the far side, with Saff and Kace.

Saff looked like some warrior queen, her dark skin gleaming and her braids falling over her shoulder. Kace was standing with his hands behind his back, watching the training with a critical eye. Like the military commander he'd been before he'd left his service to stay here with Rory.

Madeline looked sideways at Lore. "The healer said light exercise. I don't think they had gladiator training in mind."

Lore shot her one of his lazy grins. "Don't worry, *dushla*, I'll go easy on you."

They walked over to the rack of weapons that had been set out for the gladiators. Sunlight gleamed off the huge swords, giant axes, and other things she couldn't identify. That was something else Madeline had plans to learn about. Galen had a team of people who made and maintained the gladiators' weapons. She'd seen the receipts for purchasing metals, leather, and equipment, and she was sure she could optimize—

"Ah, this will do nicely."

Madeline saw Lore holding what looked like the hilt of a sword without a blade.

She frowned. "What is it?"

"Laser sword." He pressed a button and a bright blade of light shot out.

She blinked. "Wow. Um, what happens if I touch the blade?"

"It isn't set to full power. You'll get a faint burn—" that grin again "—and a hell of a sting." With an experienced move, he spun the sword and it made a faint humming sound. "It's light, and should be easy for you to use."

She took the weapon gingerly. It was far lighter than she'd imagined. She moved it slowly through the air.

Lore grabbed another large hilt. The blade on his laser sword was also blue, but longer than hers. He looked a picture of the perfect galactic gladiator: tall, handsome, and strong, a high-tech weapon in hand.

He gestured her over to a clear spot on the sand. "We need to get you used to the sword, and to loosen up your muscles. Follow my moves."

He started to swing the blade through the air, going through what was clearly a set of moves he knew by rote. His big body moved gracefully across the sand, and, for a second, she just stood there, mesmerized.

"Madeline? Move your sword."

Right. She shook her head and followed his poses.

At first, she felt stiff and awkward, but she was surprised to find herself relaxing into it. It was nice to be outside exercising, the sunlight on her back. She'd been working on space stations so long, she was used to running on treadmills in small station gyms. And then she'd spent a very long time locked in a Thraxian cell.

Her muscles warmed up, and soon she was moving the laser sword more fluidly. Lore halted to correct her a few times.

Finally, he called a stop, and she retracted the blade, grinning. "I was getting good." She pushed her sweat-dampened hair back. "Very good."

"Don't get ahead of yourself. How about we move onto something more challenging?"

Desire ignited in her blood. Madeline could never refuse a good challenge. "What did you have in mind?"

"A sparring match."

Madeline paused. He was bigger, stronger, and more experienced. She assessed their strengths and weaknesses, just as she would have done if she'd been facing a hostile crowd in the boardroom.

Lore would never hurt her. She knew that deep in her blood. Her chest tightened. Never before, not once in her life, had she ever looked at someone and known they wouldn't cause her harm.

"Okay, gladiator, you're on."

They separated, flicking their swords back on. They circled each other on the sand.

He approached, lightning-quick. Madeline barely had time to block his first swing. He was so fast. Their swords sizzled where they touched.

"Remember, you need to focus on your opponent," he said. "Every fighter gives off some clue when they are about to attack. Look for those, anticipate."

Nodding, she stepped back, bouncing a little on

the balls of her feet.

She launched herself at him. He easily blocked her hit and spun. She felt an electric sizzle at the small of her back. Like the nip of ants.

"Ouch." She turned, frowning at him.

He grinned. "You need to move faster."

Determination filling her, Madeline focused. They sparred, attacking and blocking, spinning and dodging. Perspiration ran down her face. His blade touched her a few more times, each hit making her angrier and more determined. She was going to get a hit in if it killed her.

"Ahhh." She lunged wildly and he moved, her weapon inches away from him.

"Don't lose your temper," he said, spinning.

She bit back a retort. He was right. She dragged in a deep, calming breath. She just hated losing.

She attacked again, their swords striking. She knew he'd be anticipating her to go high, because that's what she'd been doing so far. Instead, she tried the unexpected and went low.

Her laser sword nicked his side, and she heard him hiss out a breath.

"Got you!" Madeline retracted her sword, and threw her hands in the air like a champion. "I did it!"

"So you did." Lore threw his head back and laughed.

Everything in Madeline went still. It was such a good sound—deep and rich. She liked the sound of it. Her eyes went straight to his throat, the strong lines of him.

Damn. Against her better judgment, she liked him. Really liked him.

"Come on, gladiator," she said. "Don't get lazy. I want to hit you again."

With a smile, he lifted his sword. "Just a little more. Don't want you to overdo it."

She moved, careful to watch his feet and how the muscles in his legs tensed. That was where she could read his next move. "Don't tell me you're afraid?"

With another laugh, he lunged forward. They sparred a little longer, Madeline getting in one more hit while he got in two. On her ass. Her bottom was stinging a little by the time he led her over to the arched walkway, where a table of drinks was set up.

"Here." He held a glass out to her.

She took a sip of the water, thankful that she didn't feel the burn in her stomach today. God, she had to admit she felt good after that workout—skin flushed, muscles limber, energy zinging through her veins.

Then Lore reached out, his thumb rubbing across her cheek. She froze.

"You have some sand here," he said, his voice deep.

She stared into his silver eyes, and that far-too-handsome face. "I told you that you're not my type."

"I remember."

"You have all kinds of beautiful women throwing themselves at you in the arena. You don't need me."

"You're probably right."

But he didn't move away, and the heat of him licked at her skin.

Dammit all to hell. Madeline reached out, grabbed the leather straps on his chest, and yanked his mouth to hers.

Chapter Seven

Lore's tongue demanded entry, and Madeline let him in, their tongues colliding. She sank her hands into his thick hair, lapping up the taste of him. Desire throbbed between her legs, and soon, the kiss took on a wild edge, their tongues dueling. She moaned, feeling the need to devour and be devoured.

"I'd heard the healers recommended light exercise," came Galen's voice from behind them. "However, I'm not sure this is what they had in mind."

Madeline squeaked and tried to pull away, but Lore held her still, taking his time to finish the kiss with a final nip on her bottom lip that made her moan again.

Finally, Lore lifted his head and looked over Madeline's shoulder. "You should try it, G."

Galen snorted. "I have a message for you. From Vashto and Cerria."

Madeline straightened and turned to face the imperator. Her heart had lodged in her throat. "What does it say?"

"Well, they snuck it in, trying to ensure I wouldn't discover it." Galen's tone expressed how he felt about that.

"I made you out to be a pretty scary guy," Lore said, grinning.

"I am a scary guy," Galen said. "They've invited you to a party tonight, at the Glass Palace near the District." He held up a small medallion stamped with an image of fighters. "This is your invite."

"Glass Palace?" Madeline asked.

Galen nodded. "It's a large building made entirely of glass. There's a legal fight ring in there. They usually hold showy boxing or wrestling matches for the tourists."

"The fights are usually rigged," Lore added. "Glitzy fighters with fake, ostentatious moves." He sniffed. "Not really fighting."

"They said you're welcome to take one guest," Galen added.

Madeline spun back to Lore. "Take me."

"No." His face hardened. "I don't trust Vashto or Cerria. I don't want you anywhere near them."

"You've already staked a claim on me in front of them. They'll be expecting me."

"They're dangerous."

"I'm not a delicate damsel, Lore. I have a brain and I can use it."

"You're not well. Not functioning at one-hundred percent."

She thrust her hands on her hips. "I feel much better today, thanks to you."

"I didn't like the way Vashto looked at you."

"Well, I didn't either. And I especially didn't like the way Cerria looked like she was going to take a bite out of you. But we'll be there together."

"She does have a point, Lore," Galen said, although he didn't look too happy about it. "They've seen her with you, and you didn't act like she was just an arena flutterer. I suspect the addition of a guest was so you'd bring her."

Lore cursed.

"I have to find Blaine." Madeline pressed her hands against Lore's chest, desperate for him to see how important this was to her. "Please."

"Drak!" He shoved his hands through his hair.

"I'll stay by your side. We'll watch each other's back."

Suddenly, he gripped her chin, forcing her gaze up. "Only as long as you promise to do everything I say and follow my lead."

Madeline sniffed. She didn't blindly follow anyone else's orders. "We'll see."

He scowled. "You always have to try to be in charge."

"The party is tonight," Galen reminded them. "You'll need outfits. From what I hear, it's a pretty glitzy one."

Lore nodded. "Fine. Let's do this."

Galen nodded. "And you're only there to gather intel and get an invite to the underground fight rings. Do not take any risks or do anything dangerous. Understood?"

"Understood," Lore answered.

After the imperator left, Lore moved so fast, Madeline gasped.

He backed her into the stone wall, caging her

with his body. "I will keep you safe."

She pushed against his chest. Of course, he didn't budge an inch. "I'm not yours to keep safe, Lore."

"Yes, you are." He pressed his lips to her throat. "You just haven't accepted it yet."

Madeline felt traitorous heat flood her, his lips warm and wet on her skin. She couldn't find any words.

"We will be together, Madeline. You will writhe under my hands and sigh under my mouth. You will moan when I slide my cock inside you and cry out *my* name when you surrender your pleasure to me."

"Arrogant and overconfident alien," she snapped, even as she shuddered with delicious pleasure at his words.

He stepped back and shot her a charming smile. "Was that a curse or a compliment?" He stroked his hand down her side. "Get used to the idea of us, and get used to the idea that I will protect you and keep you safe, no matter what."

Madeline just stared at him, her mouth dry. Inside she was a confused mass of conflicting emotions. The one thing she knew, but couldn't say aloud, was that a part of her liked—really liked—everything he'd just said.

Lore took another step away. "I'll see you tonight."

***

Lore tugged on the cuffs of his evening shirt as he walked into the living area. The black fabric had a shiny sheen to it—just a little flashy and perfect for this party.

He heard the click of a woman's shoes and looked up.

His mouth went dry. Madeline walked toward him wearing an amazing gown. The blood-red fabric looked like liquid and draped over her curves. As she walked, a large slit appeared, baring one slim leg all the way to her thigh. She'd done something to her face, eyes lined with smoky black and her lips red. Her dark hair was slicked back.

His hands curled into fists. Want, desire, and vicious need slammed into him. He didn't want anyone else to see her. This had nothing to do with rescuing her or helping her. Right now, Lore just wanted her.

"Ready?" she asked.

He managed a nod. "You look...drak, I can't find a word to do you justice."

The slightest touch of color filled her cheeks. "Thank you."

"I have a gift for you." He reached out, drifting his fingers over her bare shoulder. He fiddled with the slim strap of her dress.

She raised a brow. "Are you going to pull it out of the bodice of my dress?"

"No." He flicked his fingers and held up his closed hand. "Do you want your present?"

She sniffed, acting like she was indifferent, even as a covetous light filled her eyes. "Well, you've already given me flowers and a coin. What's left? I'm pretty sure you can't find chocolate from Earth."

"Chocolate, huh? I'll see what I can do. But for now, this will have to suffice." He opened his palm.

Madeline gasped, her gaze on the gorgeous bracelet made of sparkling silver and red jewels.

"How did you know I was wearing red?" She lifted a hand, but didn't reach for the piece of jewelry. "Lore, I can't take it."

"Of course you can. It's a gift. Free of strings and expectations. I just thought it would look beautiful on you and complement your outfit."

She blinked and looked up at him. "No one's given me jewelry before."

Lore lifted her wrist, and slipped the bracelet around it. He closed the clasp. As he'd guessed, it looked perfect on her.

Then he frowned. "You were married. Rory tells me jewelry is a requirement when you get married."

"I'm not sure you should take everything Rory says seriously. But yes, it is common for partners to give each other jewelry, particularly rings, when they marry. But Wade and I were very young and we didn't have much money. Sometimes it was hard just to put food on the table, let alone think about jewelry." She stroked the bracelet. "After Jack got his new heart, and I got him and Wade set up in a nice house, I bought some jewelry for myself." Blue eyes met his. "But no one's ever given it to me as a gift. Thank you."

He cupped her cheek, stroking the strong line of her jaw. "You're welcome." He held out his arm. "Shall we go to the party?"

She dragged in a deep breath and nodded. Galen and Nero met them at the door to wish them luck.

"Any problems, we'll come for you," the imperator promised. "Raiden and Nero will be monitoring the party."

Nero nodded in agreement. "Any hint of trouble, we'll be there."

Lore slapped his fight partner on the shoulder. He always knew Nero had his back.

Madeline was quiet as he led her through the tunnels. Soon, they stepped out of the arena building and into the city of Kor Magna. They came out of an exit right near the District. Gleaming buildings speared into the sky, blinking with lights and advertisements for all kinds of vices and pleasures. Lore saw colored strobe lights arching through the night sky and heard the noise of transports whizzing through the busy streets.

Kor Magna was a city of contrasts. From the ancient arena and the lower-tech, cobblestone back streets where the locals lived, to the high-tech glitz and glamor of the District.

Madeline was taking in the District with an assessing eye. Lore tugged her down another side street. "The Glass House is on the edge of the District. Close enough for the tourists to find it, and far enough for it to feel like the tourists are getting a taste of the 'rougher' side of Carthago."

They passed lots of people walking the streets, a

mix of locals and tourists. They were wearing everything from fighting leathers, to simple robes, to party outfits fancier than Lore's and Madeline's. Some were heading for the casinos, others rushing to catch shows and parties. He saw quite a few men, and even a couple of women, give Madeline a second glance. Especially that drakking slit in her dress.

They turned a corner and Madeline slowed. "Wow."

Ahead, was a large building made entirely of glass. It rose up to an angular roof made of sheets of glass, and it was easy to see the crowd of people inside, and the large boxing ring in the center, where two huge men were busy pummeling each other.

He led her to the entrance, showed his invitation—a small medallion stamped with two fighters mid-swing—and they entered the Glass House.

The place was packed and music throbbed. Servers dressed in black moved around passing out drinks and food. There were some tables and chairs dotted around, and a mezzanine level ringing the room, allowing spectators to get a better view of the fight ring. Everyone was laughing and drinking.

Lore flagged down a server and murmured an order to the man. A moment later, he returned and handed Lore two drinks. Lore slipped the man a coin.

Madeline eyed the dark liquid warily.

"It's called Ronia nectar. It'll be soothing for your stomach."

He watched as she sipped it, her eyes widening as the sweet flavor hit her. Lore sipped his own and glanced around the room. Then, his gaze made contact with Cerria's bright-yellow one.

Vashto and Cerria were holding court at a table in the center of the party, not far from the boxing ring. The couple were surrounded by partygoers, all vying for their attention.

Cerria waved her clawed fingers, gesturing them over, her gaze raking over Lore's body. He'd always been able to find something attractive about any woman, but Cerria left him stone cold. He saw Vashto watching them as well, his hot gaze on Madeline.

"We've been summoned," he murmured.

Madeline barely hid her grimace. "I guess that means it's showtime."

They waded through the guests and reached Vashto and Cerria.

"Welcome, gladiator," Vashto rumbled from his seat at the table. Cerria was sitting on the table beside him, wearing a tiny dress.

The woman instantly leaped up, her claws biting into Lore's arms as she jerked him closer. She pressed herself against him, and over the throb of the music, he heard her words. "I want to fuck you, gladiator. I want to bite and scratch you, and leave you bleeding."

Nice. "It's a pleasure to see you, too, Cerria."

She leaned forward and licked his neck. He took

a step back, claiming a seat at the table and tugging Madeline into his lap. He liked that much better, except that her slim leg was on display, and Vashto was staring at it.

With a pout, Cerria leaned closer, pressing her small breast against his shoulder, her breath hot on his ear. "I will fuck you."

"Not tonight." Not ever.

"How much?" she demanded.

She was determined. "I'm not for sale."

Her eyes narrowed. "Everyone has their price. Even your pretty little flower here would have a price." Her gaze raked over Madeline.

Madeline sipped her drink, curling into Lore. "What I want, you can't give me. And unfortunately for you, Lore doesn't want you."

Cerria's gaze sparked fire. "He wants you, but I can tell you haven't fucked him yet. So maybe you don't want him enough. Maybe there's something more you want than him."

The woman turned away, shouting for more drinks.

Lore pressed his lips to Madeline's ear. "You okay?"

She nodded. "We're here for a reason. An important reason. I can put up with that catty bitch any day."

They stayed there for a while, pretending to enjoy themselves. Cerria laughed loudly, touching any male within reach. Vashto drank steadily.

Then Lore stood, setting Madeline on her feet. Vashto eyed them.

"I want a closer look at the fight." Lore wrapped an arm around Madeline.

Vashto nodded. "Enjoy the party and all its entertainments." His gaze moved to Madeline again. "I'll be in touch."

Lore nodded and pulled Madeline into the crowd, eager to put some distance between them and the couple.

They moved through the party, the music turning from a thumping beat to something with screeching strings. There were pockets of people dancing, and others shouting and cheering for the boxers in the ring.

Lore saw her glass was empty. "I'll get you another drink. Stay right here."

She nodded, her gaze on the fighters. Lore turned around and took a few steps to order with the closest server.

When he turned back, he saw a giant, red-skinned, horned alien towering over Madeline. She appeared to be telling the man to leave her alone and waving him off.

But the alien stepped in closer. His skin color deepened and the curled horns on his head started to glow.

That's when Lore saw Madeline go stiff, her face frozen.

Fear. She was keeping her face blank but Lore saw below that mask of hers now. Realization burst inside him. The alien was a Gnashian, a distant relative of the Thraxians.

The alien grabbed her arm and she twisted,

trying to jerk out of his hold. Lore charged forward, fury boiling inside him. He knocked several people out of his way.

"Leave her alone." He grabbed the man's arm.

A second later, the Gnashian gave a loud yell. He released Madeline and stumbled away.

There were two perfect scorch marks of Lore's hands burned into the alien's arm, and Lore's hands still flickered with flames.

Chapter Eight

Lore cut off his power, and hoped no one saw his veins glowing gold beneath his skin.

"Go." He glared at the red-skinned alien. "Before I hurt you far worse than that."

With a strangled noise, the Gnashian hurried off. Lore wrapped an arm around Madeline, pulling her away from the crowd and toward the darker edges of the room.

Back near the entrance that led down into the kitchens below, he pulled her close, turning his back to the crowd. "Are you okay?"

She nodded, her gaze still on his arms. In the shadows, the fading glow of the veins in his arms was more noticeable.

"He frightened you."

"I know. It was stupid. He just reminded me of the Thraxians." Her gaze met his head-on. "The fire…it's not just an illusion."

Lore stiffened. Was she afraid of him? He was so used to keeping his ability secret, he wasn't sure what to say.

She reached out and grabbed his palm, turning it over and studying it. She traced her fingers up his arm. She didn't appear afraid. "How do you do it?"

"Males are rare among the Nomi for a reason. We have...extra abilities."

"Pyrokinesis." She shook her head. "And the water during the show yesterday...you were really manipulating it. It should be impossible."

"For humans and most other species, yes."

Her gaze was steady. "But not for you."

"No, not for me. Or rather, the males of my species. We are born with the mental ability to control the movement of molecules in our body. Like water molecules. And we can also speed up their movement in order to increase the temperature."

"And create fire," she breathed.

He pulled her closer. "It's always been kept a secret by my people, Madeline. Nomi males are believed to be extinct, and in the past, when people heard of one alive, he was usually hunted, killed, or dissected."

She was silent for a moment, her gaze running over his face. "You've been hiding a part of yourself."

"I'm not hiding, Madeline, but I don't broadcast my abilities either. I'm a member of the House of Galen now and that gives me certain protection." He cupped her cheek. "For you, I'm an open book. I'm certainly not hiding how I feel about you."

"We're a bad idea, Lore." Her breath hitched. "I'm a mess. Inside, I'm just shattered pieces."

He leaned closer, letting his breath wash over

her cheek and her scent sink into his senses. "Then let me help you put those pieces back together."

He touched his lips to hers. Just a gentle nip. Her lips parted, her hands sliding up to his shoulders—

"I wasn't expecting to see anyone from the House of Galen here this evening."

The smooth male voice made Lore lift his head, and he bit back a frustrated groan. Why did everyone interrupt him when he tried to kiss Madeline? The elegant man standing nearby with his hands in the pockets of his expensive black suit was watching them with an amused half-smile. The man's black hair was tied back at the base of his neck.

"Rillian."

The man inclined his head. "Lore, it's a pleasure to see you." The man's black gaze flickered silver as it landed on Madeline. "And you must be Madeline Cochran."

"I am," she answered.

"Madeline, this is Rillian, owner of the Dark Nebula Casino, and a friend of the House of Galen." He was careful to keep Madeline close to his side. Rillian was handsome, suave, and rich. He was also known for enjoying beautiful women.

"A pleasure, Madeline." Rillian turned back to Lore. "Since I know Galen detests these fake boxing matches, and Vashto and Cerria, I'm very surprised to see you here."

"I didn't think this was your crowd, either," Lore said.

Rillian lowered his voice. "I got wind that they might have news on the underground fight rings. Terrible business. I'd like to do anything I can to help shut it down."

Lore relaxed, but only a little. Rillian was an ally, but Lore was smart enough to recognize deadliness, even when it was coated with a high gloss. "We're here for the same thing. Galen invited Vashto and Cerria to an arena fight, and I ensured they issued me an invite tonight."

Rillian raised a dark brow. "If they're interested in you, they'll be interested in getting you to fight."

"Yes." And lead them to Blaine.

"Our friend is stuck down there in the fight rings," Madeline added. "He's being forced to fight to the death. We have to find him before it's too late."

The casino owner nodded. "A few of the wealthy elite are talking. Vashto is making the rounds, one by one, and handing out tickets to a select few for an exclusive event."

Madeline sucked in a breath. "A fight? When? Where?"

"I don't know yet. He hasn't talked to me, but apparently, he just finished talking to Sile."

Lore grimaced. Sile was an ugly, crude reptilian who owned several casinos in the District. "I've heard all kinds of nasty rumors about the man...including that he likes to eat people."

"Unfortunately, I've heard the same things." Rillian glanced at Madeline and then back at Lore.

"I know Sile has a thing for pretty, smooth-skinned women."

Madeline straightened her shoulders. "If you get me an introduction, I'll talk to him and find out what he knows."

"No," Lore said.

"You'll be right here, watching me. If he tries anything, you have my permission to rescue me. I'll be perfectly safe." She lifted her chin. "Besides, this is my decision, not yours."

"You promised to follow my orders."

"No, you just demanded that I would."

Rillian was watching them with a half-smile. "I'd be happy to give you an introduction." He looked at Lore. "And I'll help keep her safe."

"Where is he?" Madeline demanded.

Rillian pointed discreetly to the left of the boxing ring. Lore easily spotted Sile sitting with a group of his goons. He had cracked reptilian skin, large eyes, heavy brow ridges, and an elongated jaw that accommodated his sharp teeth.

Madeline grimaced. "He looks like an upright crocodile. You shouldn't use my real name. How about—"

"Maddy," Lore suggested. "Close to your real name so you won't slip up."

Her nose wrinkled. "I hate Maddy, but fine, it'll do." She ran her hands down her sides. "Wish me luck."

Lore yanked her into his arms and pressed a hard kiss to her lips. "Do not get hurt. Not a single hair."

Her eyes softened. "I won't, Lore."

Reluctantly, he let her go. Madeline glanced at Rillian.

"Let me gain his attention first. Then you can introduce me." She sauntered toward the alien, her hips swaying in a sensual dance.

Lore's hands clenched into fists. He hated this.

"Another gladiator falls at the dainty feet of a woman from Earth," Rillian said.

"Call her dainty to her face, I dare you."

Rillian smiled. "Oh, no. I know these women are fierce under their soft, small bodies."

Lore forced himself to take a long, calming breath. "Go. Introduce her and keep her safe. Anything goes wrong, and Sile won't be the only one to feel the edge of my sword."

Rillian inclined his head, and followed Madeline.

Lore stuck to the shadows, but moved as close as he could to where Sile was sitting. Most of his guards were reptilian as well, but from a variety of species. He saw the instant the man noticed Madeline walking through the crowd, his gaze zeroing in on her.

A moment later, Rillian appeared by her side and Lore could tell Sile wasn't very happy about that. When Rillian nodded to Sile, the reptilian waved them closer.

Madeline smiled a sultry, come-hither smile at the alien.

It made Lore realize that she'd never smiled at him like that. He watched her walk into Sile's little lair, and he cursed.

One wrong move, and Lore would snatch her up and get her out of there.

***

Madeline stared at the ugly creature.

His skin looked like parched earth, cracked under a dying sun, and while he had a humanoid shape, she could see a long tail. His long mouth was full of teeth, but his eyes—green with a large elongated pupil—held intelligence. And were cold…so very, very cold.

"Rillian," Sile drawled, his voice deep and husky.

"Sile. Enjoying the party?" Rillian sat on a couch and Madeline sat beside him.

"Not nearly as much as you must be with this delicious creature by your side." His eyes stayed locked on Madeline.

"Sile, this is Maddy. She is a friend of mine."

Madeline forced a smile. "I asked Rillian to introduce me. I hear you're an important man." She edged closer to Sile, ensuring the slit in her dress fell open. If he liked smooth skin, she'd make sure he got an eyeful.

"Where are you from?"

"All over." She smiled again, trying to think of this just like any meeting she'd been to where she'd needed her poker face to keep her true feelings hidden. "You own casinos." She let her voice turn breathy.

"I do, sweet thing."

Did he mean sweet to look at or sweet to taste?

Ugh. It unsettled Madeline's stomach to think of him eating people. "I like casinos, but gambling is...boring." She pouted.

"Boring?" Sile said, surprised.

"It's monotonous. Like I always tell Rillian, I like more...action and excitement. I love going to the arena to watch the fights."

Sile grunted. "There are bloodier shows than the arena."

"Oh?" She feigned surprise. "I can't imagine that." She licked her lips, and Sile's reptilian gaze moved there.

"Yes, sweet thing. I know of one coming up." He leaned forward, touching her thigh. "Right here."

"Here?" She looked at the boxing ring. "This is just a silly boxing match."

Sile shook his head. "Not in this ring. *Beneath* it."

Her eyes widened. "Wow! Beneath here?"

"I'm assured it will be a fight to rival all fights."

"When?"

He shrugged. "I haven't been told yet. Rillian here doesn't have a ticket, but I do." Sile's chest puffed out. "I could get you in...as my special guest."

She saw hunger in his gaze now, but for the life of her, Madeline couldn't tell if it was sexual or physical appetite.

Not in this lifetime, ugly. "I think I'd—oh—" she pressed a hand to her stomach, feigning pain "—I'm sorry, I need the restroom. Now!"

Sile frowned. "Are you ill?"

She waved a hand at him. "Oh, it's nothing. I just recovered from a nasty illness. Couldn't keep anything in. It was coming out at all ends." She widened her eyes and clapped a hand over her mouth. "I think, I think..."

Sile looked alarmed now, waving her off. Rillian grabbed her elbow and they hurried away, Sile's guards parting fast to let them through.

"Nice job," Rillian murmured as the crowd swallowed them.

She straightened. "Thanks. And thanks for your help." She scanned around for Lore. "We got the information we needed."

Rillian nodded. "As far as I know, there is nothing below the Glass House except the kitchens."

Where the hell was Lore? "Well, I guess that's why these guys are so good at hiding the fight rings."

Suddenly, strong arms wrapped around her from behind. There was no time to panic, and she recognized Lore's strength straight away.

"Thanks, Rillian."

The casino owner nodded and stepped back. "If I hear anything else, I'll let Galen know." The man walked away.

Lore dragged Madeline back to their dark corner near the kitchen entrance. Far away from Sile.

"Are you all right?"

She nodded. "The guy is creepy. But he gave me the information we needed. There's a fight planned...right beneath the Glass House."

"Beneath? There's never been any talk of anything beneath the Glass House." He scanned the room. "Galen will look into it."

She huffed out a breath. "I wish we knew more."

"It's a good start."

The door to the kitchen swung open nearby and some servers walked out holding loaded trays.

Lore stroked her hair. "Are you sure you're okay?"

"I'm sure. Sile was definitely interested in me, but I couldn't tell if he wanted to kiss me or serve me sautéed."

"You're safe now."

The door opened again, but this time, it wasn't kitchen staff who exited. It was three big, burly aliens. The men were all laughing.

Something pinged on Madeline's radar, and it must have done the same for Lore, because he pulled her deeper into the shadows. Then he pushed her up against the wall, pressing his body against hers like they were two lovers having an illicit tryst. He pressed his lips to her throat and she tightened her hands on his shoulders.

But his body was taut, his attention on the men.

"The Srinar are busy organizing the fights. The human and the beast will be the star attractions. Can't *wait* to see them tear into each other. Nothing civilized left in either of them."

"I want to see that human guy with the dark skin fight," another man said. "Guy's vicious!"

"The tattooed, blue alien is good. He's stronger, wilder."

"The other guy is smarter and faster."

As the men moved past, Madeline got a faint whiff of stench. Like these guys had been somewhere that smelled horrifically bad.

"I also hear the Srinar have a *dag'tar* lined up. They are sneaking it in tomorrow," one of the aliens added, excitement in his voice. "I've never seen one before."

"Talk about vicious. I've heard those creatures rape their prey before they eat it!"

"I heard the Thraxians gave the Srinar some more of those Earth women to set loose with the *dag'tar.*" Sick pleasure rode the alien's voice. "We'll see how they fare."

The laughter of the guards disappeared into the noise of the party.

"Women?" Lore whispered.

Madeline's heart hammered in her chest. She was in shock. She couldn't believe what she just heard. "I never saw any other humans. Only Blaine."

"Well, it sounds like there are more women down there, and the Srinar are going to feed them to a *dag'tar.*"

"Which is what, exactly?"

"It's the worst sort of creature you could imagine."

Madeline swallowed. "Well, we can't let this happen to whoever they have captive down there."

Lore's face turned considering as he stared at the kitchen door. "I have an idea."

Madeline frowned. "Galen said no risks."

The door opened again and two servers rushed out. Lore took a step toward them. "I have a really good idea."

Chapter Nine

Lore dragged the two unconscious bodies of the servers back into the kitchen entry area. Thankfully, there was an area where the servers stashed their personal belongings, and they weren't visible to the main part of the kitchen.

He took a moment to strip the black uniforms off of them, then dumped the bodies inside a cupboard. He tossed one set of clothing at Madeline.

Lore turned and pulled the too-tight jacket on. Behind him, he heard the whisper of fabric as Madeline slipped out of her dress. He sucked in a breath. He was a gladiator and a man used to getting his own way. And he wanted Madeline Cochran. He turned his head.

Blue eyes met his. "A gentleman would keep his back turned."

She was naked, except for two tiny wisps of underwear that looked like the finest of netting. She slipped the jacket on, covering her gorgeous breasts.

"I'm not a gentleman," he told her.

She snorted and pulled the trousers on. They were far too big, and she took a second to cinch them in. The jacket would hide the fabric gathers.

After stashing their clothes in an empty cupboard, they headed down some stairs and into the main kitchens.

The area was bigger than Lore had expected, and busy. Servers and chefs of numerous species were moving to and fro. By the far wall, a row of chefs were busy preparing the food, steam wafting into the air.

Lore nodded his head, and he and Madeline moved deeper into the kitchen area. He scanned the room, but didn't spot anything that looked like entrances leading to secret underground fight rings. There were pantries and storage rooms, with kitchen staff bustling in and out.

Frustrated, he stopped. They couldn't risk asking any of the workers. Suddenly, Madeline grabbed his arm, her fingers squeezing.

"Look," she murmured.

Off to the right, against the wall, two big aliens were coming out of a room marked 'storage.' The man and woman didn't look like kitchen servers or chefs. They looked like hired muscle.

Lore and Madeline waited until the aliens had moved off, and then hurried in that direction. They stepped through the doorway, and instead of a storage room, they found a set of stairs leading down into darkness.

He grabbed Madeline's hand and they headed down.

"Galen isn't going to like this," she whispered.

"Just a quick look around, and then we'll get out."

She nodded, and when they reached the bottom of the stairs, they found themselves in a dark tunnel lit by infrequent lights set into the walls.

"Doesn't look new," Lore mused. "In fact, this tunnel looks pretty old."

They hadn't gone far when a foul stench slammed into them.

"Oh, God." Madeline squeezed her nose, revulsion on her face.

The reek was unimaginable. The tunnel came to an end at a closed door in the wall. Lore cautiously pushed it open.

It was an entrance to the sewers.

"Someone must have repurposed some of the old sewer tunnels," Lore said.

"Charming."

"Let's go a bit farther." He pulled out a towel stuffed in the pocket of his server jacket. He passed it to her, and she pressed it to her nose.

"What about you?"

"I can decrease my sense of smell."

"Handy skill to have right now."

They headed into a larger tunnel. It was round, with a walkway on one side of it. The rest of it was filled with a river of dark, murky water that stank.

Keeping to the walkway, they followed the tunnel's twists and turns. Soon, they reached a junction where the tunnel branched off in two directions.

"Look." Madeline pointed to some half-dried footprints on the ground, heading off to the left. They followed. They passed a few alcoves that were clearly designed for the storage of sewer-maintenance equipment.

Moments later, Lore heard the echo of voices moving toward them. *Drak.* They couldn't be caught down here. How far back was it to the last alcove? He glanced ahead and spotted one not far away.

He grabbed Madeline's hand and yanked her forward. She stumbled, but kept up with him. He slid into the tight space, pressing his back against the rock wall. He slid down, and pulled Madeline into his lap. They were wedged into the small space, barely hidden by the shadows.

Madeline tilted her head, clearly listening to the guards getting closer. He felt her tense, and then she shifted a little, her round bottom brushing against him.

Lore pressed his mouth against her ear. "Is it wrong that I'm turned on right now?"

Her breath hitched. "Yes. The stench is horrible."

He nuzzled her neck. "I can only smell you."

"Shelve the charm, Lore," she whispered. "Now's not the time."

"Only if I can use it later. And my tongue. It's a clever one."

She sniffed. "I wouldn't know."

He grinned to himself. "Let me show you."

"Shh! They're nearly here."

The voices were louder and now he heard the clank of chains.

The guards moved past, herding a prisoner

between them. Madeline's gaze was locked on the guards, revulsion crossing her face. Both guards were Srinar—with tumor-like growths on their faces caused by the plague that had decimated their species and set them on a path to becoming scum of the galaxy.

Then Lore looked at their captive. The man was made of ropes of hard muscle, no fat on him anywhere, and skin darker than Madeline's. His chest was bare, and crisscrossed with ragged scars. He wore torn, filthy trousers. His black hair was shaggy, and he had a face that looked like it was hewn from the stone around them.

Madeline gasped quietly and Lore pressed a hand to her mouth.

"Blaine."

Her lips moved against Lore's palm. So this was the man from Earth. He was far bigger than the females.

"Move it, Earth scum." One of the guards jammed a fist into Blaine's side.

The man moved fast. Faster than Lore thought possible. Blaine spun and thrust a fist into the guard's face. It was brutal, violent, and hard. The guard flew backward with a cry, and fell into the mucky, foul water.

The other guard moved forward, snapping out a stun baton. He slammed the device into Blaine's gut, and a flash of blue electricity lit the tunnel. *Drak.* Lore pulled Madeline closer, praying they weren't exposed.

Blaine's body jolted, all his muscles straining,

and his teeth snapping together. He dropped to his knees.

The first guard dragged himself out of the water, his body dripping, a dark scowl on his face.

"Don't antagonize him, Taoul. I've lost track of how many guards he's killed."

Both guards flanked Blaine, grabbing his arms, and dragged him away.

"I'm going to enjoy watching you fight the *dag'tar*," the wet guard snapped. "It'll tear you apart with its giant cock." The guard let out a nasty laugh. "They're going to toss the females in with you. Make you watch what it does to them, first."

Lore's jaw clenched. This was beyond depraved. While fights in the arena above could get wild and bloody, no one was killed. But this…

"Come on." Madeline stood and slipped out of the alcove. "We have to gather more intel."

Lore followed her, and they snuck deeper into the tunnels. Not far ahead, the tunnel ended, and they stepped out into a giant cavern.

This looked natural. Lore studied the rock walls of the circular space, lit by burning torches. He looked upward and noticed a faint circle of light far above. "They must have used the sewer system to link up with the underground caves and sinkholes." Carthago was riddled with caves.

They hugged the wall and ahead, he saw cells carved into the walls with metal bars.

"That way." Madeline pointed. They left the wall, moving quietly across the large space.

She moved ahead, toward a darker area in the

center. The lighting in the cavern was sporadic at best, the place draped in darkness. But as she took another step, Lore realized what he was seeing.

"Madeline, stop!"

She took one step, not realizing the darkness was a giant hole. She made a strangled sound, starting to pitch forward. Lore grabbed her and yanked her back.

Down below, a beast roared.

"Jesus." She clung to Lore, staring down in horror.

He heard something moving around deep below, grunts and snuffles echoing up, but it was too dark to see what it was.

Then Lore looked across the hole at the rock wall. It was honeycombed with cells, all covered in bars.

And in the closest one, he spotted three women, huddled together on the dirty floor.

"Look."

Madeline stared across the gap and took a sharp intake of breath. "They're definitely human."

"Do you know them?"

She shook her head. "I've never seen them before."

Voices echoed behind them, accompanied by footsteps. *Drak.* "Someone's coming! We have to go."

But Madeline tugged on his hand. "We have to get the women out."

"We can't. Not now. We'll come back." He grabbed her arm and yanked her back toward the sewer entrance.

"Hey, what are you doing here?" an alien guard yelled at them.

Drak. Slowly, Lore turned. Three big alien guards were bearing down on them.

They were all as tall as he was, and broad across the shoulders and chest. One had faint green skin, while the other two were some sort of reptilian race.

He tensed, getting ready to fight. He wished he had his sword right now. He could take them, but it wouldn't be pretty, and it was going to hurt.

Then Madeline stepped forward. "We just delivered food to the other guards. Do you need anything?"

One of the reptilians let out a grunt. "Mutaba knows he isn't allowed to get servers down here. Lazy drak needs to collect food from the kitchen himself."

Madeline glanced at Lore, before she bowed her head. "As you wish."

Lore quickly lowered his gaze and followed her lead.

"Get out of here before Vashto or any of the Srinar catch you."

Madeline elbowed Lore, and together they turned and calmly walked back to the sewer entrance.

Lore's pulse was racing. He was used to fighting his way out of every tough situation. But Madeline's quick thinking had saved them a hard fight.

He glanced down at her as they slipped into the tunnel. "You were brilliant."

She smiled up at him. "I know. Now, let's get the hell out of here."

***

Once again wearing their party clothes, Madeline and Lore hurried back to the safety of the House of Galen.

Adrenaline was still pumping through Madeline's veins, and she was so glad to be out of those stinking sewers.

Galen and the others met them just inside the door.

Thorin's nose wrinkled. "You reek."

"Impromptu trip to the sewers," Lore told him.

"We saw Blaine." Madeline looked at Harper. "He's alive."

Galen stepped forward, frowning. "You weren't to snoop around, only gather information from Vashto. If you'd gotten caught—"

"We were caught." Lore smiled. "Some of Vashto's guards caught us, but we were dressed as servers, and Madeline was magnificent. She got us out of there."

Galen raised a brow, eyeing Lore's broad shoulders. "They bought you as a server?"

"There's something else," Madeline said, her voice hardening. "We saw three other human women locked in a cell."

She saw Lore scowl. A hard look she'd never

seen on his face before. "They have a *dag'tar*. They're planning to toss the women and Blaine in the ring with the creature."

Galen hissed out a breath. The imperator turned and slammed his fist into the wall. "Drakking scum."

"What's a *dag'tar*?" Harper asked.

"The worst of the worst of creatures to fight," Raiden said.

"*Dag'tar* males have a very high sex drive," Thorin said. "Fighting gets them worked up."

Harper grimaced, then looked at Madeline. "Who were the women? Were they from Fortuna Station? Anyone from Security?"

Madeline shook her head. "I didn't recognize them. I knew everyone aboard Fortuna, and none of these women were familiar. Of course, it was dark and they were filthy, so it was hard to know for sure."

"It doesn't matter," Lore said. "No one deserves this fate. We'll get them all out."

Saff stepped forward. "So, what's next?"

"A covert operation to the sewers." Galen's dark gaze took them all in. "But first, we'll need maps so we can plan the mission. We can't enter through the Glass House, so we need an alternative entrance point."

"That'll take some time," Raiden said.

Madeline ground her teeth together. "They don't have time. The Srinar and Vashto could schedule this fight at any time—"

"And I won't send my gladiators in unprepared

and get them all killed or caught."

Galen's sharp voice made her snap her mouth closed. Frustration ate at her with hungry teeth, but she nodded.

Galen ran a hand over his head and looked at her. "You go and get cleaned up, Madeline. Good work tonight."

She knew when she was dismissed. With a nod at the others, and then one last glance at Lore, Madeline hurried to her room. She stripped off the dress. She touched the soft fabric, sorry the gown was ruined. She couldn't imagine that anyone could get the stench out of it.

Naked, she stepped into her adjoining bathroom and into the shower. She let the water pummel her, and she soaped herself up numerous times until her skin and hair smelled like citrus, not sewer.

Once she'd dried off, she pulled on her sleep shirt. It had been a long night, and she needed some rest. She glanced at her big, comfy bed, and thought of those women on the hard-packed floor.

The smell was gone, but the images weren't leaving. That terrible place, the cells, the guards. Blaine and those poor women exposed to who knew what.

Madeline was too wound up. When she'd felt like this on the space station, she'd jumped on the treadmill, or she'd worked. She needed something to do. Something to organize or fix or rearrange.

She pulled on some soft shorts, and headed out to her new office. When she stepped into the room just near Galen's, she felt something inside her ease a little. Just the sight of the desk and bookcases made her feel better.

She flicked on a small lamp on the corner of her desk and it cast a warm, orange glow around the room. The desk wasn't large, but it gleamed. She stared at the stack of files she'd left sitting on it. The pages contained numbers on some new medical equipment Galen was considering for Medical.

That's what she could do—she'd go over them now. Anything to keep her mind off those poor captives.

At her desk, she lifted the files, opening the first one.

"You should be sleeping."

She looked up and saw Lore leaning in the doorway. He'd showered, his hair damp, and his chest bare. He wore soft trousers that draped his hard body and left little to the imagination.

She swallowed, forcing her gaze to his face. "I can't sleep. Not when I know that those women and Blaine are stuck down in that horrible place."

"You're supposed to rest when you can, Madeline. Healers' orders."

He stalked closer, and her heart thumped. Suddenly, she felt very much like prey in the presence of the big, dangerous predator.

"I've always sucked at relaxing."

Something flashed in his eyes. "I have a few ideas."

Heat curled through her. Then, without warning, he reached for her, tugging her against his chest. His mouth took hers—hard, possessive, and hungry. With a moan, she kissed him back, her fingers digging into his shoulders.

His lips slid away from hers, nipping at her jaw and going lower. One of his big hands cupped her breasts through her shirt.

"I want you, Madeline." He flicked at her nipple, making her arch. "I want to touch, taste, and pleasure you. Is that what you want?"

"Lore." Her voice cracked a little, desire pooling low in her belly.

His teeth locked on her neck, and she cried out. He backed her up and, a second later, she felt her desk behind her. He pushed her back onto it.

When she looked up, she saw stark hunger in his gaze, those eyes more silver than gray.

"Tell me yes, *dushla*." His fingers hooked in the sides of her shorts. "Tell me you want me."

They stayed there, caught together, the moment taut like a bow. Her chest squeezed tight, all the air caught inside her.

It came out in a rush. "God, yes, Lore. Please."

At her words, he yanked her shorts off in one fluid move. Then he was nudging her thighs apart with his wide shoulders. He shoved her shirt up, baring her breasts. His hot gaze moved over the heaving swells, skimming down her stomach, to the center of her. He was looking at her like he was committing it all to memory, like he owned her.

No one had ever looked at her like this. No one had ever made her feel so beautiful or wanted.

He palmed her between her legs, fingers running through her curls. With a strangled cry, she arched into his clever fingers. Then he lowered his head.

As his mouth closed over her, she bucked her hips, her head falling back. His tongue licked at her and he growled against her, a wild, sexy, satisfied sound. He settled deeper, lapping and sucking at her.

Madeline clamped her hands on his head. It was too much, and not enough. Heat was a firestorm burning through her.

His mouth found her clit, licking it once before he closed his mouth on it. She jerked against him, crying out with each suck.

He pressed a big hand to her belly, holding her down, and kept working her. He made a low sound, like he couldn't get enough and wanted more.

Madeline moaned, her body strung tight and filled with a bright mass of sensation.

"Let yourself go, Madeline." He nipped at her inner thigh. "You're safe with me."

He plunged two fingers inside her, his mouth sucking hard on her clit.

With a wild cry, her release crashed over her, like the brightest supernova. And held safely by her gladiator, Madeline let herself fly apart.

Chapter Ten

The taste and feel of Madeline was driving Lore out of his mind.

He growled, still lapping at her. He watched the pleasure shake through her body and color flood her cheeks. As her sexy body bowed up, laid out for him like the prettiest of offerings, he luxuriated in her pleasure.

She'd trusted him. She'd given herself to him.

When she finally subsided, lying on the desk, body sprawled in abandon and her chest rising and falling fast, he leaned over her, hands braced either side of her body.

"What do you want next?" he demanded.

She licked her lips. "I want you."

"What do you want to do with me, *dushla*?"

"I want to pleasure you."

"How?"

She reached out, running her hand down the center of his chest. "Like you did to me. With my mouth."

His cock throbbed at the thought. His gaze dropped to her kiss-swollen mouth.

He straightened and pushed her back down. He circled the desk, running his hand over her naked body. She was gorgeous, with her smooth skin and womanly curves. He stopped near her head, tipping it back over the edge of the desk. She watched him, upside down, and he slid his finger into her mouth. She sucked on it, and the heat in him reached unbearable levels.

Quickly, Lore shoved his trousers off. His swollen cock sprang out, and he slowly rubbed it across her lips. She opened her mouth and he slid it inside.

She made a hungry sound, and started sucking.

Drak. So wet and tight. Lore squeezed his ass, thrusting forward into her delicious mouth. She never took her gaze off him as she worked his cock furiously.

"Enough." On edge, out-of-control, Lore pulled out.

He grabbed her and spun her around until she was facing him, her bare bottom sitting on the very edge of the desk. He cupped her breasts, feeling the tantalizing weight of them fill his palms. He teased the pink nipples to hard points, loving the sounds she made. He leaned down, sucking one nipple into his mouth.

Madeline cried out, grinding against him, her hands tangling in his hair.

Finally, he lifted his head and pushed her legs apart. He gripped his cock, rubbing it against her folds. "Watch."

He saw her gaze drop to his heavy cock. Tension hummed between them.

"What do you want, Madeline?"

"I...you..."

"Say it. What do you want me to do?"

Her hips bucked, trying to get him inside her. "Fuck me. I want you to fuck me, Lore."

He pressed the mushroom head against her, and slowly, ever so slowly, he pushed inside her. She moaned.

"Tell me how it feels," he growled.

"Big. Solid." Her voice was strangled. "I feel so full."

She felt so good and tight around him. Unable to stop, his control evaporating, Lore slammed inside her.

She cried out, her ass moving on the desk. As he hammered into her, her arms gripped him for an anchor, her nails scratching down his back.

"Yes," she cried, her hips pumping against him.

"Come for me again, Madeline."

She moaned again, her body starting to shake. She was getting close and from the heavy sensation gathering at the base of his spine, so was he.

He kept sliding into her. "Your body's milking me, *dushla*. You're going to make me come deep inside you." He gripped her hips, feeling her body tense up. "That's it, Madeline. Come apart for me now."

Her body shook harder. "Oh...oh..." Her hot gaze met his.

Staring into her eyes, he watched as her orgasm hit, her eyes widening. He held her shaking body, slamming home one last time.

With a roar, Lore poured his release inside

Madeline, feeling her clawing at his shoulders. *Drak.*

He collapsed forward, trapping her against the desk, his almost violent release leaving him hot and stunned.

***

Madeline lay stretched out on the desk. She was dimly aware of the cool surface beneath her naked body, and extremely aware of the hot, hard male lying on top of her.

Every muscle in her body was lax and languid, heat still ebbing in her belly. The only sound in the room was the sound of Lore's harsh breathing.

He moved, pressing a kiss to her belly. She quivered.

"Stay here," he ordered.

She heard him yank on his trousers and his footsteps as he walked away. She lay there for a moment, but then started to feel exposed. She'd had a lot of offices during her career, and she'd never once been naked in any of them. Let alone naked and stretched out on her desk after being thoroughly fucked.

She was just sitting up when Lore reappeared in the doorway.

He was carrying a tray.

He set the tray down on a small table by the lone couch in the office. It wasn't the prettiest couch, covered by some rough-looking brown fur. Lore turned, scooped her off her desk, then settled himself on the couch, arranging her in his lap. He picked up a steaming cup off the tray and handed it out to her.

"A cup of Ar'bor tea."

She sipped the delicious drink. The man was a gladiator, through and through, but he really enjoyed taking care of others. That protective streak was the width of the galaxy.

Next, she watched him pick up a small vial. He tipped it onto his hands and she saw a clear oil. The scent of musk and wood filled the room.

"I bought this off Regan. It's her latest batch of massage oil."

He nudged Madeline forward, then his hands were at her neck and shoulders, massaging deep. A small moan escaped her mouth and her chin fell to her chest. He found the knots of tension and pressed his thumbs into them. The man had very clever hands. She wondered how many women they'd pleasured.

"Stop thinking," he whispered. "Just for tonight."

One night of bliss sounded amazing. But Blaine and those women didn't have that luxury. "I need—"

"There's nothing you can do right now. You need to switch it off sometimes, Madeline. It helps you cope."

"It's not like flicking a switch or pressing a button. It's not that easy."

"No, it's not, but you have to work at it. I'll help."

The hands kneading her shoulders slipped over her front, cupping her breasts. She arched back against him, barely noticing when he took her empty teacup and set it aside. He played with her nipples until her breasts felt swollen, her nipples tight. Then one big hand slid down over her belly and between her thighs.

She opened her legs, her breath hitching, and he found her clit.

"So fascinating, this little nub." He rolled it between his fingers.

Soon she was gasping and rocking on his lap. Beneath her, she felt the hard press of his cock through his soft trousers.

Madeline was on fire. When he slid one finger inside her, thrusting deep, she cried out. She could barely contain the sensations rocketing through her.

Sex had never been like this before. So much sensation, so many feelings.

His mouth nipped at her earlobe, his teeth scraping over her neck. "Stop thinking."

"I can't." Her mind never shut down.

"Yes, you can. And now I want to hear your cries as you come on my fingers."

"I can't come again." But she felt another release teasing her, shimmering just out of reach.

"Don't deny me, Madeline."

"I only ever come once, Lore."

"You've already come on my mouth and cock, so I know that's a lie. And Raiden, Thorin and Kace have mentioned some interesting things about women from Earth." He slid two fingers back inside her, stretching her.

Madeline made an incoherent noise. "We aren't all the same. Every woman's different."

"You will come for me again." His tone was firm. This was the determined gladiator under the charming showman. He hid it so well, that it was easy to forget.

But her release stayed stubbornly out of reach. She made a frustrated sound.

Suddenly, he was on his feet, carrying her forward. He crossed the distance to her desk and pressed her face down onto it, her hips hitting the edge. One big palm rested between her shoulder blades, while his other hand nudged her legs apart.

"Surrender to me, Madeline." A hot, sexy whisper. "Give your pleasure over to me."

She made a noise, feeling Lore's fingers running through her wet folds.

"It's just you and me here." His teeth raked down her spine. "And I want to make you feel so good."

"I...I can't."

She knew she held on to everything too tightly. She liked being in charge, in control, always making things fit right. Maybe she liked it too much, but all that had been taken away from her when she'd been abducted.

Lore's palm came down and connected with her buttock with a sharp, shocking smack. Madeline cried out, rearing up. But he held her down. It hadn't been hard enough to hurt, but it did sting.

"Let go, Madeline." He hit her other cheek. He gave her a few more slaps and soon all Madeline was thinking about was the warmth and sting across her bottom.

"Lore." A choked cry. "Please!"

"My good little *dushla*."

She heard the rustle of fabric, and then his thick cock was sliding inside her.

The relief made her cry out. She needed him so badly.

But he didn't give her a chance to adjust. His fingers gripped her hips and then he was thrusting into her—hard and fast and rough.

Madeline heard someone crying out and begging for more. Oh, God, it was her.

As Lore thrust again, her orgasm ripped through her. She cried out his name, could do nothing more than feel. She heard his long groan as he poured his release inside her.

She'd been lost for so long. But right here, right now, she felt found.

***

Lore could get used to this.

He was lazing in the giant tub in his bathroom. The hot water felt nice on his skin. He'd grown up on a spaceship, traveling from world to world. He hadn't been able to indulge in long baths and had to make do with short showers.

Madeline walked into the bathroom wearing a silky black robe. She looked hesitant, her eyes uncertain.

He sighed. He could practically see the thoughts

turning through her head. The only time this woman switched off that busy mind of hers was when his cock was deep inside her. "Get in, *dushla*."

She fiddled with her robe, then unbelted it and let it fall to the floor.

Praise the stars. He could look at her lovely body all day long. The intriguing dips and flares. Those dark curls between her legs. The intriguing dark spot on her left breast she called a mole.

She stepped into the bath. "Ouch, it's hot."

"Sorry. That's how I like it."

She sat, keeping some space between them. Lore snorted. He'd busted down the barriers that she used to keep the world out, so he wasn't letting her rebuild them again. He yanked her to him, water sloshing. She gave a startled squeak.

Turning her, he settled her between his legs, her head resting back against his chest. He started playing with her dark hair.

It took her a moment, but finally she relaxed back against him.

"I know Galen had a meeting this morning with the other gladiator houses," she said. "He should be back soon, right?"

"Yes. But it'll take however long it takes. Trust takes time." Lore reached down and stroked her slim leg. He knew that better than anyone.

He heard her breath hitch. He knew she didn't realize it, but she was incredibly sensitive to his touch, and he loved that. There was so much passion locked away inside this woman, and he wanted to help her set it free.

He trailed his fingers higher and she closed her legs, trapping his hand.

"I enjoyed last night," she said primly, her muscles tightening. "Thank you."

Lore rolled his eyes toward the ceiling. "It was my pleasure."

"As long as you understand that this is just sex. A biological response."

"Oh?" He hated hearing her say that. It was strange, usually he was the one telling a woman that they were just having some fun. He pressed his fingers into her tense shoulders, massaging the knots of tension. When she tried to stifle her moan, he smiled.

"I think you enjoy a variety of women," she said. "You have quite a smorgasbord of easy offerings."

"You aren't easy."

Now she went stiff, turning her head to look at him. "So why are you here?"

"Because you fascinate me, Madeline." He reached out, fingering her damp hair. "Because this isn't just sex."

Her eyes flashed. "Lore—"

"Because I've been in your position, your entire life destroyed, and I have to say, you're coping a lot better than I did."

"I don't feel like I am."

"One day at a time."

She leaned back against him. "I liked it when I was in control of my life. When I knew what I was doing and I felt like myself."

"*Dushla*, I think I should tell you that you're in control here, as well. And you always seem to know what you're doing."

She froze, considering that, her gaze turning inward. Had she not realized how much she was doing around the House of Galen? How much she was helping in the search for Blaine?

Lore traced the shell of her ear and pretended to pluck out something. He held it out to her. A beautiful blue jewel the same shade as her eyes.

"It's lovely." She stared at it but didn't touch it.

"Just take it."

For a second, he was sure she was going to argue with him. Then she snatched it.

Then she really surprised him, turning in his lap to cup his cheeks. She yanked him forward for a deep kiss. It only took a microsecond for fire to thrum through his veins.

"I never expected anyone like you," she whispered.

Those quiet words broke his heart. He knew what she really meant. That she never thought she deserved someone who cared about her. He pressed his mouth back to hers. He deepened the kiss and had them both groaning.

He rested his forehead against her. "Unfortunately, we have a meeting to go to, to get maps to the sewers."

She pulled back, her gaze sharpening. "A meeting with whom?"

"With the information merchant."

Her eyebrows rose. "The mysterious Zhim."

"He's really not mysterious. More annoying than anything. But yes, we're meeting him at the spaceport. Apparently, he's doing work there."

Madeline shot to her feet, water sluicing off her body. "Then let's get going."

Chapter Eleven

Lore regretted leaving the nice, warm bath, and he regretted even more watching Madeline pull clothes over her naked curves. They strode into the living area where Raiden and Nero were waiting for them. Raiden was wearing his red cape and Nero wore a leather harness across his chest, topped with gray fur.

"Ready?" Raiden asked.

Lore nodded, watching Nero's gaze move between him and Madeline. Yeah, it was pretty obvious what he and Madeline had been doing. "Any word from Galen?"

"Still locked up with the imperators," Raiden answered.

Lore snatched a cloak from a nearby closet and held it up to Madeline. "Wear this." The gray fabric was trimmed in red, and fastened with a medallion embossed with the House of Galen logo. "It marks you as House of Galen, and will give you some protection."

She nodded, letting him clip it on. He stayed close to her as they left the arena and headed out into the city. As they stepped out into the morning sunshine, he watched Madeline take a second to lift her face to the sky and close her eyes.

He knew that she'd been kept in cages and ships for months, and it would take a long time for the memories of that to fade. He grabbed her hand, pleased when she let him, and they followed Raiden and Nero into the city streets.

Away from the towering spires of the District, the buildings of Kor Magna were simple, two-story buildings all made of local stone. During the day, the streets were filled with locals going about their business—working, heading to the underground market, herding their children to school. At night, it was a different place. People locked themselves in to avoid the dangerous gangs that roamed the darkened streets.

Not that anyone would mess with gladiators. Especially not House of Galen gladiators.

Soon, they reached the Kor Magna Spaceport. The area was cordoned off by a high, metal fence. Beyond the wire, rows of ships of all different shapes and sizes were visible. Off to the left sat a large building made of graceful arches—the main spaceport terminal.

They set off toward the terminal, when he noticed Madeline had stopped. He followed her gaze to a black, spike-covered ship sitting in the distance.

A Thraxian slaver ship.

He touched her shoulder. "Okay?"

She pressed her lips together and nodded. "Yes. For now, I'm focused on Blaine, those women, and whoever else is trapped down in the fight rings."

Her gaze swung back to the Thraxian ship. "But really, our ordeal isn't over until the Thraxians are stopped."

He had no love for the slavers, but even though they were enemies of the House of Galen, the slavers—and their species in general—were still powerful and connected. "One battle at a time, *dushla*."

When they stepped inside the terminal, people of multiple species were bustling in all directions, despite the early hour of the day. Monotonous voices were announcing arrivals and departures of different spaceflights, and offering tours to nearby planets.

Madeline stared. "It's such a contrast to the ancient feel of the Kor Magna Arena. In here, it almost reminds me of our space station." Sadness flitted over her face.

Lore grabbed her hand. They moved through the busy waiting area, and soon were heading through a doorway and into a corridor leading to the back rooms of the terminal.

Finally, they stepped into a windowless room filled with beeping equipment, comps, and electronic screens. Seated in the middle of the chaos was Zhim.

The man's tall, lanky body was sprawled in a chair, and he was wearing a multi-colored shirt that mirrored his unique eyes. He had an angular face and dark hair pulled back in a messy knot at the back of his head. He smiled at them, though Lore noticed the expression did not reach his eyes.

"Raiden, Nero, and Lore, welcome." Zhim greeted them, but his gaze was on Madeline, sharp and interested. "And Madeline Jane Cochran. Civilian commander of the Fortuna Space Station. Rising star at the Axis Corporation."

"Former commander and former employee." Her tone was one Lore expected she used on hapless employees on her space station. "And you're the infamous Zhim."

The information merchant stood, spreading his hands. "I am." He tilted his head. "I thought you'd look taller."

Madeline tilted her head. "I thought you'd look...smarter."

When Zhim frowned, Lore snorted to hide his laugh. Raiden was grinning, and even Nero's lips quirked up at the edges.

"We've come for the sewer maps," Lore said.

"And I just confirmed that the payment Galen sent me cleared." Zhim held out a small, slim-looking chip of translucent material. "Everything's on there." Then Zhim's face changed, turning uncharacteristically serious. "Be forewarned. The sewers are a bad place. A tangle of confusing tunnels, with who knows what living there. I've heard bad, but unsubstantiated, rumors of dangerous things down there in the shadows."

"Scared of the dark, Zhim?" Nero asked.

"No. The only thing that scares me is a lack of information."

As Raiden clipped the chip into the portable comp he'd brought with him, Lore noticed Madeline was looking intently around the room.

"What is all this?" she asked.

Zhim smiled, seemingly pleased that someone was showing an interest in his stuff. "Some of my equipment. I send and receive messages through the spaceport's relay station. We have a nice little working agreement. Let's just say, I enhance their equipment and they let me piggyback on their system. It means I can get information not just from Carthago, but from other planets in the system and beyond." His eyes gleamed.

"Impressive," Madeline said. "How far?"

"Not to the other side of the galaxy, I'm afraid."

Her interest visibly dimmed, and she nodded.

"Not yet, anyway." Zhim circled around some equipment and pointed to a screen filled with information and diagrams. "But I'm working on it."

Madeline leaned forward, frowning at the screen. "This is information on wormholes." She looked over at Zhim.

He nodded. "I'm currently investing a lot of time, energy, and money working on some new wormhole technology. My dream is to pull information from *all* over the galaxy."

"How?" she demanded.

Lore watched as Zhim's face softened a little, as if the tech geek almost felt sorry for Madeline. Lore touched her back. He knew how desperately she missed Jack.

"I have some of my people working on generating micro-wormholes, so I can transmit and receive messages through them."

Madeline shook her head. "Generating wormholes takes a hell of a lot of energy."

Zhim nodded. "But I'm only talking about a very long but very, very small wormhole. Just enough for data. Yes, it takes a lot of energy, so it's expensive, but I won't give up until I achieve it. Imagine…information from all over the galaxy!"

"A wormhole through space-time, directly to another point." She considered it. "But how do you guarantee that you'll transmit your messages to the right time? You could end up sending them to the past or the future."

Zhim shrugged. "Still working on it. But I'm also intrigued by the thought of sending information back to the past or gaining information from the future." The man's eyes gleamed.

Lore crossed his arms over his chest. "You mean *sell* information from the past and future. Some sticky ethics there."

"I've never let ethics worry me," Zhim said with a sharp smile.

"But you think you can control the timing of your messages?" Madeline said.

"I like to believe that anything's possible, Madeline." He tilted his head. "What would you tell your son?"

She swallowed visibly, and Lore wanted to punch the information merchant.

"I'd tell him what happened, and that I'm alive and that I love him."

"Thanks for the maps." Raiden slipped his comp back into his pocket. "Keep this between us, Zhim."

"Always." Zhim's multi-colored eyes met Lore's. "Be careful down there."

Lore tilted his head. "Getting soft, Zhim?"

The man sat and picked up some wires. "Of course not. I just don't want to lose one of my best customers."

Madeline was quiet as they headed back to the House of Galen. Lore was worried. During their night together, she'd opened up, and he'd hoped she was closer to accepting her new life here at the House of Galen. With him. But talk of Earth and wormholes had opened up her wounds again.

Once they reached the House of Galen, Galen was waiting for them. He gestured them all into his office, and any sign of sadness on Madeline's face was gone, replaced with a focus on the mission at hand.

Galen stood in front of the window, his hands clasped behind his back. "The Houses are still considering my proposal to join forces and shut down the underground fight rings."

"For a bunch of gladiators, they seem pretty indecisive," Madeline said.

He speared her with a sharp look. "They are cautious about risking their best fighters and making dangerous enemies."

"We have the sewer maps," Raiden said.

Galen nodded. "If we have better information on the fight rings, it will help sway the other imperators. Where are they exactly, and what is down there."

"When do we go in?" Madeline asked.

"We?" Lore felt every muscle in his body go tight. He shook his head. "A team of experienced fighters will go in."

Madeline ignored him. "I'm a part of this. I'm going."

Galen spun. "Again, this is *my* decision. I'm imperator of this house." The man's voice held an edge, and everyone in the room stiffened.

Madeline lifted her chin. "If you don't take me, I'll find another way to get down there. Blaine worked for *me*. I was in charge of the space station, and ultimately I failed him and the others by letting them get abducted." Her gaze touched Lore's before circling the room. "I appreciate all your help. For giving us all refuge here, for helping to rescue us. But I *need* to be a part of this."

"No." Protecting her had gone beyond just a want or need. It was deep in Lore's blood now. He snatched her up, and when she started to kick and wrench away, he held her tighter.

"Lore—"

He ignored Galen's warning tone and focused on Madeline. "I will keep you safe, even from your own stupid decisions."

She struggled. "What are you going to do? Lock me up? Drug me?"

Lore froze.

Her face spasmed, and her voice turned to a harsh whisper. "Please don't be like my nightmares."

Instantly, his gut turned to stone, and he set her down. He was horrified to think she'd consider his need to protect her to be anything like what the Thraxians had done to her.

"I'm starting to realize I'm not broken." She gave Lore a long look, before turning back to Galen. "I'm dented a little bit, but I'm not broken. I've been down in those sewers, and I can help find Blaine."

"This will be a scouting mission, to gather more information to help us convince the other houses to join us in the rescue. We will not engage." Galen's icy-blue eye turned to Lore. "She can come, and you will keep her safe."

Lore wanted to argue. His hands flexed. The protective need deep inside him wanted to list all the reasons it was safer for her to stay behind.

"I'm not a precious little thing for you to coddle and protect," she said.

"You won't look after yourself, so someone needs to do it for you."

She set her shoulders back. "Well, consider yourself off the job. I *can* look after myself. I always have." She stomped out.

Lore closed his eyes. *Smooth as Bollian silk, Lore.* He released a breath and opened his eyes. His friends were watching him.

"You can't lock her up," Raiden said.

"How can you stand it?" Lore asked them. "How can you stand to watch your women heading into danger?" He knew they'd all done it.

Thorin lifted a big shoulder. "You have to stand with her, support her, and even though she won't want it, be her shield when she needs it."

Kace nodded. "You can't just lock her away from

life. She's already had that done to her."

Raiden slapped a hand to Lore's shoulder. "Help to give her what *she* needs, Lore. Not what *you* need."

Chapter Twelve

Madeline finished dressing in the black leather clothes Harper had brought her. She looked at herself in the mirror. The trousers, shirt, and vest fit pretty well.

It felt good to *do* something. Her belly was churning again at the thought of heading back into danger, and at the thought of Lore.

No. She was *not* thinking of Lore.

There was a knock at the door. When she opened it, she found a house server bringing a tray of food for her.

"This was ordered for you." The woman placed the tray on a small table and left with a small nod.

Madeline stared at the food. The tray was filled with fresh foods, a bowl of steaming broth, and a milk drink. All things that were good for her stomach. She knew exactly who was responsible for sending it to her. She stared at the meal for a second, fighting the childish urge to not eat anything. Then, she picked up a crusty hunk of bread and dipped it in the broth. She needed the fuel for the mission ahead.

Soon, there was another knock at the door. Harper stood in the doorway, wearing similar black clothing to Madeline's. But Harper's leather trousers molded to her muscular form with loving familiarity.

"Ready?" Harper asked.

Madeline nodded. "I am."

They walked down the corridor together. "This is a simple in and out," Harper said. "We head in, assess the guard numbers, get the layout and situation, and get out."

Madeline swallowed. "And then we find a way to get Blaine and the women out."

"Still no idea who they are?"

Madeline shook her head. She'd mulled over the mental picture she'd taken, but none of them had looked familiar.

"It doesn't really matter who they are." Harper's voice was steady and strong, like the woman herself. "We won't leave them there."

Madeline suddenly grabbed Harper's arm. "Harper. I was never nice to you."

The former space marine cocked her head. "We never really knew each other."

"I didn't let people get to know me."

Harper gave a nod. "I get it. It's hard being the boss."

Madeline released a breath. "It wasn't just that. I'd shut myself off."

A smile flirted on Harper's lips. "Well, I think a certain gladiator has put a stop to that."

Madeline wasn't going anywhere near that comment. "Anyway, I just wanted to apologize."

"You might have been a little bit tough and

harsh, Madeline, but I never doubted you'd do the right thing for the space station and the people on it. There was nothing you could have done to prevent the Thraxian attack. And now you're doing the right thing for Blaine and those women."

When her eyes prickled, Madeline fought back the stupid threatening tears. "Thank you, Harper. For everything."

Together, they stepped into the living area. The gladiators were already gathered. Immediately, her gaze went to Lore. The man looked so damn good dressed all in black. He was looking at her, and she quickly turned away to face Galen.

"Zhim found us an alternate entrance into the sewers," Galen told them. A map flashed up on the screen on the wall. "We'll be going in here." He pointed to a glowing orange dot.

There were murmurs and nods.

The next thing Madeline knew, she was sandwiched between Raiden and Harper as they left the House of Galen. They moved quietly through the darkness of the sleeping city, passed darkened houses and closed storefronts. The bright lights of the District glowed in the distance.

The part of the city they traveled into looked more industrial and more run-down than the rest she'd seen. Large stone warehouses cast immense shadows, and she saw furtive movements in the darkness. The gladiators kept together as a tight group, weapons raised.

Then a smell hit Madeline. It was like running into a wall, and it made her gag. She'd thought the sewers were bad, but this was a hundred times worse.

"Tanneries," Raiden told her. "This is where they tan leather for use in the arena."

Madeline held her hand to her nose. She couldn't even describe the foul stench. Maybe rotting fish combined with dead things.

Ahead, large vats had been carved into the rocky ground. There was an entire grid of them, gleaming under the moonlight. Some were filled with whatever chemicals were used in the tanning process, while other vats were empty.

They passed the tannery area, Galen checking his small comp screen.

"Makes sense to have an entrance to the sewers here," Lore said. "The place already stinks."

Galen lead them down a narrow alley between two tannery buildings. A round, metal manhole was set into the ground. The imperator gestured, and Nero and Thorin stepped forward.

It took the giant gladiators some grunting to lift the heavy cover up. They tossed it to the side with a clang.

A dark hole yawned at them.

Galen crouched, flicking on a small, hand-held light. "There's a ramp heading downward."

Madeline watched Galen drop into the hole. The others followed. When it was her turn, she crouched near the edge and took a breath.

Hands grabbed her, and she stifled a yelp as she was lifted down. She glanced up at Lore. "I didn't need the help."

His face stayed impassive. "Of course, you didn't."

She turned away from him. It was so dark, and now the stench of sewer was competing with the fading stench of the tanning area.

"Drak, I won't be able to smell for a week," Thorin complained.

Galen lifted a hand, and they moved down the ramp. Soon, it leveled out, and they walked through a few inches of murky water and sludge. Madeline blocked all thoughts of what was actually in the water from her head.

Moving deeper, she saw small shadows racing away from them. Rats, or the alien equivalent, she guessed. Strange sounds echoed through the tunnels, and they set her nerves on edge.

Soon, they were so deep in the twists and turns of the sewers, she knew she'd be lost without the map. Suddenly, Galen stopped, lifting a hand.

They were at the end of the tunnel and ahead of them lay a giant lake of mucky, noxious water.

"The cavern you saw below the Glass House should be just ahead," Galen said. "Just on the other side of this reservoir."

Madeline spied a narrow walkway of rock that crossed the center of the lake.

"Let's go." Galen went first.

Madeline stepped out on the walkway, trying not to think about slipping into the dark water. The lights they were holding cast only enough light to see a few feet in each direction. She had no idea how big the lake was or how deep. For a second, she wobbled, and Lore grabbed her arm to steady her.

"Careful," he murmured.

She looked at him for a moment, his handsome face partly hidden by the shadows. Damn him for being so attractive. She was still mad at him for his arrogant, alpha-male behavior earlier. And she certainly wasn't going to tell him she had that pretty blue gem he'd given her tucked into her pocket for good luck.

Madeline focused on slowly and steadily crossing the lake. Soon, they were all on the other side and passing through another short tunnel.

They came out on a ledge ringing the large sinkhole cavern. They were up much higher than the level where Madeline and Lore had been on their other visit down here.

As Galen and Raiden crouched near the edge, she stared down, noting the cells on the far wall, and the deeper hole that housed the *dag'tar*.

Voices echoed up from below, and the gladiators all stepped back, pressing their backs to the wall. Lore pulled her close to his side and she elbowed him in response, but she kept her gaze on the guards walking into view below.

She heard a quiet click, and saw that Galen was taking pictures with some sort of device. Dimly, she heard the gladiators' hushed whispers, as they discussed tactics and numbers. She searched for any sign of Blaine or the women.

"There," she whispered. "The women."

The three women were out of their cell, being

pushed by guards. One woman—a tall brunette with long, curly hair—spun, and must have said something to the guards. The next instant, one of the guards backhanded her, sending her sprawling.

Madeline gasped and felt all the gladiators around her tense. But she knew that up here, they were too far away to help.

Get up, Madeline mentally urged the woman. *Hold on until we come for you.*

The woman stood, her two friends moving in close to her.

"My God, there's Blaine," Harper whispered.

She saw him now, covered in chains, guards prodding him as they urged him toward a cell. He was covered in blood and gore. Madeline pressed a hand to her chest. She guessed that he had been brought back from some sort of training fight.

Then she heard another noise—a thumping sound of flesh on metal, and the roar of an angry beast.

More guards came into view, dragging a giant metal box behind them. The metal box had several small holes in the side of it.

"Careful," a guard yelled, his voice echoing upward. "Don't get too close to the box."

"He's just a drakking beast," another guard answered.

Madeline frowned. Surely the box was too small for a *dag'tar*?

"He's not just a beast. He was a man once, but he's been locked up and made to fight for years. There's nothing left but a mass of rage, but he's far smarter than any animal."

"I don't think so." A squat, stocky guard stepped forward and banged his stun baton against the box. Then laughing, he shoved the baton through one of the holes in the box.

An enraged roar echoed from the box, raising goosebumps on Madeline's arms. Beside her, Lore muttered a curse.

Suddenly, there was a large thump. The box vibrated, rocking to one side. The three guards froze.

"I told you to be careful," the first guard snapped.

The box jerked again, the side denting outward under the force of a blow.

"Drak!" the stocky guard yelled.

More hits hammered the box, and the guards backed up.

Suddenly, the box burst open, the metal splitting like paper.

A man...creature...alien burst out. He stood for a second, chest heaving. He had a large, powerful body, with dark-blue skin covered in swirls of dark tattoos. Long, dark, tangled hair covered most of his face, but even from a distance, it was easy to tell he was staring at the guards.

The three men took a few halting steps backward.

The beast-man attacked. Screams echoed upward, and with three brutal blows, he took the guards down.

He let out another roar, lifting his head. The

sound reverberated deafeningly off the rocks.

What the hell was he? And what had been done to him?

And that's when Madeline realized something else had caught his attention, his huge body going still.

He was looking at the women.

The human women were huddled together, watching in horror. Their two guards stood, shaking, beside them.

The blue alien moved fast. He rushed across the space in a charge worthy of a linebacker. He picked up one guard, spun him, and tossed the man through the air. He slammed into a rock wall, before tumbling to the ground. The other guard simply dropped his weapon and ran.

The tall brunette stepped forward and pushed her friends behind her. She lifted her fists, never taking her gaze off the blue beast.

"We have to help them," Madeline said frantically.

"We can't get down there from here," Galen bit out. "We're too far away."

Suddenly, Blaine flew into view, dragging his chains behind him. He crashed into the blue alien, knocking the beast-man to the ground.

Soon, both fighters were back on their feet. Blaine swung one of his chains above his head. The alien rose slowly, his black tattoos appearing darker on his blue skin. The beast-man let out a roar.

Blaine let out his own yell and slammed the

chain toward the alien. "Get back!"

Madeline realized he was shouting at the women. Protecting them.

Suddenly, there were more shouts. A huge group of guards burst out of a tunnel, heading toward Blaine and the beast.

Blaine dropped his chain and stepped backward, closer to the women.

The blue alien turned, lifting his giant fists. One of the guards tossed a net device.

It exploded, tangling over the beast. Then it lit up, and blue electricity ran over the alien's skin. The beast roared in pain, his body jerking. Madeline pressed a fist to her mouth, feeling a streak of sympathy for the creature. Whoever he was, he'd never deserved this.

He went down on one knee, and managed to get a fist free, clobbering a nearby guard, knocking him to the ground.

Three guards leaped forward, jamming stun weapons into the alien's body. He fell facefirst onto the ground.

Madeline forced herself to watch. They didn't give Blaine a chance to surrender, and they stunned him as well. As he fell, the women screamed.

It only took moments, but soon the guards were dragging the bodies of Blaine and the blue alien into nearby cells. The women were shoved roughly into another.

Galen watched, a muscle ticking in his jaw. "We've seen enough. Let's go."

They turned to leave, heading back into the sewer tunnels.

Madeline barely noted the stench this time, her thoughts on Blaine, the women, and even that poor alien. What had they done to him to make him like that?

They reached the lake and headed out over the narrow rock path. She couldn't wait to get out of here and wash off the stink, and then plan the rescue mission. The others moved ahead and Madeline hurried to catch up.

She heard a faint splash and felt something slide along her ankle.

What the hell? She turned to look, and didn't see anything except a faint ripple in the water. She glanced down at her foot and saw a trail of sludge on the rock path behind her.

Shaking her head, she turned to follow the others. She spotted Lore's broad back ahead. She took another step, and this time, something wrapped around her ankle with a wet slap.

She looked up, and saw Lore turn back, a frown on his face. Their gazes locked.

Madeline didn't have time to say anything or scream. With a violent jerk, she was yanked into the water.

Chapter Thirteen

Unfamiliar emotions slammed into Lore.

As he watched Madeline disappear below the dark water, he realized the main one was fear. He shouted for the others, sprinting back along the pathway.

He'd remembered the whispered rumors of mutated creatures that lived in the sewers. God, even Zhim had warned them.

"Madeline!" Without any conscious thought, Lore went to dive in after her.

Strong hands gripped his arms on either side of him. Galen and Nero flanked him, stopping him from following her.

"Let me go!"

"Wait," Galen demanded. "You won't do her any good if you kill yourself."

The sound of splashing water made all their heads jerk up. Lore's chest went hard. In the middle of the lake, giant tentacles rose out of the water, waving around the air in a frenzy.

One lifted, wrapped around a screaming Madeline. She was thumping her fists against the creature's dark, rubbery skin.

It dunked her down into the water, then lifted

her up again. Then it dropped lower again, and Madeline disappeared beneath the dark water.

Lore pulled his sword, and beside him he heard his friends doing the same.

All of them watched and waited, and a dizzying whirl of thoughts tumbled through Lore's head. He had to find a way to get Madeline out of there.

"Harper, Thorin, and I will attack it from over there." Raiden pointed to the edge of the lake closest to the creature. He ran, Harper and Thorin following close behind.

Lore glanced at Kace and Saff. "You two take the other direction. If it gets within reach, slash it." Hopefully, that would get it to drop her.

The pair nodded and took off at a run. That left Lore with Galen and Nero. They watched as the creature broke the surface of the water again, and this time he saw its yawning mouth in the center of its body. A horrible, round hole ringed with sharp teeth.

"We need to distract it," Lore snapped. "Keep its attention off Madeline until we can get her out of there."

Galen nodded, gesturing for Nero to follow him.

Lore's fighting partner caught his gaze. "We'll get her out."

Lore nodded, pulling in a shuddering breath. Then he spotted some old metal-and-wood scaffolding attached to the rocky wall beside the lake. It was rusted and rotten, maybe some sort of long-abandoned maintenance framework. A broken chain dangled off it.

As he ran toward it, he heard his friends shouting at the creature. Heard metal striking flesh.

Without thinking, Lore leaped out toward the chain. He didn't have time to test it, and he prayed it would hold his weight.

He grabbed the metal, and used his momentum to swing out over the water. Below, he saw the creature splashing. He swung closer to Madeline and caught a glimpse of her terrified face.

Lore slashed with his sword, the blade biting deep into the tentacle. Blood squirted, and the creature let out a high-pitched screech. It thrashed in the water, pulling Madeline away.

The chain swung back. *Come on*. Lore used his weight to swing back as fast as he could. On the edge of the lake, he spotted Kace and Saff working together, hacking at another tentacle that had landed on the walkway. The tentacle detached, and this time the creature's screams turned to shrieks, making Lore wince.

As he neared the creature again, he saw the tentacle holding Madeline rise up high. Then he saw it tighten around her. She screamed, but then her cry was cut off as the tentacle continued squeezing her.

Drak. It was going to kill her.

Heart pounding, Lore pulled back and then pushed off to swing out again. At the peak of his swing, he let go and dropped down on the creature's head. With a roar, he drove his sword into its rubbery skin.

The water creature thrashed, but Lore spread his arms, fighting to keep his balance. He cut at another tentacle, blood splattering.

Suddenly, yet another tentacle sprang up from behind Lore and knocked into him. He was airborne for a moment, before he splashed into the water. It wasn't very deep, and his head cracked into the rocky bottom. He came up spluttering, heart thundering, blood pouring into his left eye.

He knelt, slightly dazed, pain tearing through his head.

It only took him a second to know that nothing was broken. He pushed up and got one leg beneath him. Madeline needed him. His woman needed him.

Lore fought his way back to the walkway. A second later, another tentacle flopped in front of him, making him leap backward. Quickly, he climbed up, leaped onto the tentacle, and ran along it. It moved beneath him and he moved faster.

He'd lost his sword when he'd fallen. Now, Lore reached for the powders on his belt. He hoped their small, protective pouches had protected them from the water. He grabbed one and tossed it. The smoke exploded right in front of the creature's face, and it made a sound eerily like a cough. Then it started jerking around wildly.

Lore wrapped an arm around the tentacle, holding on, and yanked out the knife strapped to his thigh.

He heard shouts behind him and glanced back. Galen was also running across another tentacle, headed toward him. As he neared, the imperator leaped into the air. Lore's breath caught and he watched as Galen raised his sword above his head. Fierce and focused. That was Galen. He crashed down onto the creature and brought his sword down.

Lore lifted his knife and let go of the tentacle. He jumped up and jammed the blade into the creature's mouth, digging into soft flesh.

The next thing Lore knew, Saff was beside him, running with impeccable balance. She lifted her staff and slammed it down into the creature's yawning mouth.

The water monster made a horrible noise. The agonized noise of a dying creature.

It bucked violently, and it knocked them all off. Lore had the sensation of flying again, before he hit the water. He came up, murky liquid streaming off him, and saw the creature lifting Madeline up high into the air. Then, its tentacles all drooped as it died. Madeline was released, and she hit the water with a splash.

The monster sank back down into the water, leaving only a few ripples on the surface of the pool, almost as though it had never been there.

Lore ran through the water. Madeline was floating facedown, and wasn't moving.

He reached her, pulling her into his arms and turning her over. He shoved her sodden hair off her pale face.

"Madeline!" His hands were shaking. "Drak, please open your eyes."

Her eyes opened and inside them, he saw suffering.

"Lore—" It was a harsh, pained whisper, blood dribbling from the corner of her mouth.

"Hold on!" He moved toward the edge. "I've got you, *dushla*." Finally, he climbed out onto the walkway, the others there to meet him.

Galen reached for her, laying her out on the ground. Lore swallowed. Her clothing was torn in places, and he could see bruises developing, mottling her body.

Galen pressed his fingers to her neck. His jaw tightened, his icy gaze meeting Lore's.

"She needs the regen tank. Now!"

Lore lifted her lifeless body into his arms and ran.

***

Lore sat in the infirmary beside the regen tank.

The rectangular glass reservoir was filled with a thick, blue gel that facilitated healing. They were very expensive to buy and maintain, but Galen had invested in three of them, to keep his gladiators in peak condition.

The center tank held a slim, dark-haired body.

Medical was deathly quiet, except for the occasional beep of some equipment nearby.

Madeline had died.

Lore dropped his head into his hands. Only steps away from the House of Galen, he'd felt her heart stutter and her breathing stop.

Drak. She'd been floating in the tank for hours. The healers had assured him that she was alive and healing, but until he heard her voice, he couldn't quite bring himself to believe it.

They'd fought. He'd driven a wedge between them before the mission, and she'd almost lost her life.

He'd almost lost her.

He moved and felt a sting above his eye. He hadn't let the healers work on him, wanting all their attention on Madeline. Someone had cleaned most of the blood away, at least, and brought him a change of clothes. He still smelled like sewer, though.

Lore turned his gaze to the tank, watching her floating there. She looked peaceful now, but he'd never forget the sight of her caught in that monster's tentacles. And the sound of her scream as it had crushed her.

Suddenly, her body jerked. He straightened. She jerked again.

Lore raced to the tank, reaching over the edge to pull her out of the blue regen gel.

"Take it easy. I'm here. You're okay." He helped her out and into his arms. She looked a bit dazed and confused. He took the clean towel that was ready and waiting for him to use, and gently wiped the gel off her skin. Then, he pulled the blanket off a nearby bunk and wrapped it around her.

He sat back in his chair, pulling her into his lap. "*Dushla.*" His voice cracked.

"I'm okay." She shivered.

He pulled her more tightly to his chest. Somewhere, a door whispered open. A Hermia healer appeared.

"Please, put her on the bed so I can examine her."

Lore just tightened his arms around her, and stared at the healer. He felt Madeline's fingers clench on his shirt.

The healer gave a quiet sigh. The Hermia were very used to dealing with gladiators. "Very well." The healer lifted a handheld scanner and ran it over Madeline from head to toe. "Your health is optimal and your injuries are healed. You just need some rest."

With a nod, the Hermia left, and Lore tucked Madeline's head under his jaw. "Never again."

"Not your decision, gladiator," she said, quietly. "Thank you for saving me."

They stayed there for a long moment before he picked her up and carried her out of Medical. As he strode down the corridor, he spotted Harper, Regan, and Rory. The women looked like they wanted to talk to them, but he shot them a look, and they backed away. Only Rory's mechanical dog, Hero, held his ground, growling.

Soon, Lore strode into the bedroom. His.

"You're moving into my rooms," he said.

"Lore—"

"No arguments, Madeline." He strode into the bathroom and flicked on the shower. He slipped the blanket off her and helped her step under the spray. He stepped in behind her, fully clothed.

"You're mine."

"I don't belong to anyone—"

He soaped up his hands, running them over her body and hair to wash away the remnants of the regen gel. "You do." He nuzzled her neck. "I'm sorry I gave you orders. I just wanted to protect you."

He felt her relaxing slowly against him.

"I was afraid," he murmured.

He finished washing her, then flicked off the shower and wrapped her in a drying cloth. After sitting her on the edge of the stone tub, he stripped off his wet clothes and wrapped a drying cloth around his hips. He lifted her again and strode into the bedroom. He laid her down, then climbed on the bed beside her. He fitted his body around hers, holding her tight.

"I need you here," he murmured. "I need to hear you breathing. I need to hear your heart beating. I need to feel your warmth against me."

She sighed, turning to face him. "I'm fine, Lore. Perfectly healed."

He swallowed, feeling like a rock was lodged in his throat. "But for a while there, you weren't." He tried not to let the horror seep into his voice, but she must have heard it.

Her face softened. "Okay."

"Okay?"

"I'll move in with you."

He grinned, his chest expanding. He touched the delicate shell of her ear, and held out an item for her.

Madeline eyed the small, dark square.

"It's called *grezzo*. Regan tells me it tastes almost as good as chocolate from Earth."

Madeline touched the small treat. "You found me chocolate?" There was amazement in her voice.

"For you, anything."

She popped the *grezzo* into her mouth, making a small humming sound. Then her eyelids fluttered. "It's so good."

He smiled at her, touching her lips. Now, he saw her eyes droop.

"Tired," she murmured.

"Rest, *dushla*."

She dropped into sleep quickly, but Lore didn't. When she snuggled into him, trusting him, fully relaxed in his arms, his chest loosened.

He stayed there in the darkness, holding her tight. He'd fallen in love with this tough woman from Earth, with her prickly shell and her wounded heart.

Lore moved so his head rested against her chest, and fell asleep to the sound of her heartbeat.

***

Madeline opened her eyes. She felt so toasty warm.

She stared at the unfamiliar covers on the bed, and felt the unfamiliar warmth behind her.

Lore's room. Lore's bed. Lore.

She stayed there for a second, absorbing it all—the scent of him, the strength of him, and the steady sound of his breathing.

Energy hummed through her veins. She hadn't

felt this vibrantly alive in so long. Shifting against his hard body, she felt vicious need nipping at her. A need for him.

Madeline rolled over, her gaze raking his big, solid body. Every inch of it was so easy to look at, perfectly formed and honed by the arena. From the handsome face, to the muscled chest, to the tempting ridges of his abdomen.

Her gaze dropped lower, to the hard part of him that she was very interested in giving some extra-special attention.

Desire flared hot, like a supernova, and she cupped his heavy cock. She started to stroke it and then slithered down to wrap her lips around him. She loved that she had to stretch her mouth wide to take him all in. And it grew under her licks and sucks.

His body jerked. "Madeline."

She made a humming sound, drawing him deeper into her mouth. So good. The musky taste of him, the thick vein running up his cock, the groan that tore from his throat.

His hand tangled in her hair, and he pulled her mouth off him. "I need to be gentle with you, but I'm not feeling gentle right now."

"I'm fine." She rubbed against him. "I need this, too."

"You died." His voice vibrated with violent emotion. "You stopped breathing. Your heart stopped beating."

Something inside her softened. He was in pain, and she wanted to soothe that. "Lore—"

"I'll never forget that." His voice was raw, his big body trembling.

She leaned down, peppering kisses across his stomach, feeling the muscles tighten under her lips. She stroked his thick cock. "I'm alive. I'll prove it to you."

She pushed him onto his back, climbing up to straddle his lean hips. She lifted her hips, desire setting her on fire, and moved herself until she was right where she wanted to be.

Looking down, she stared into his shifting gray eyes. His hands clamped on her hips.

Madeline sank down slowly, lodging him inside her. A cry tore from her throat, and mingled with his deep groan.

"So drakking beautiful." His hands slid up, cupping her breasts. "Fuck me, Madeline. Ride me while I touch you."

She moaned, lifting herself up, then driving her hips back down. She moved around, changing angles to see what felt best for both of them. As she leaned forward, the pressure on her clit was perfect, and she sank her teeth into her bottom lip.

"That's it, *dushla*. Ride me hard." His big hands clamped on her ass, fingers digging into her buttocks, as he helped to work her up and down on his cock. "Come for me, Madeline."

Silver-gray eyes were hot on hers. Her orgasm gave her no warning, slamming into her and stealing her breath. Her back bowed, her cry silent.

Beneath her, Lore thrust his hips up, bucking into her as deep as he could. He growled her name as he shuddered with his own release.

She collapsed on him, her breathing ragged, and she held on tight. He was a fire hotter than anything she'd touched before, and she was very worried that she was freefalling into love with this overprotective alien gladiator.

And love was a risk Madeline wasn't sure she was brave enough to take.

Chapter Fourteen

Madeline had been to many meetings in her life, but never a war meeting.

All the gladiators of the House of Galen stood in the living quarters, ready and armed.

Galen pressed his hands against the table. "I got word from Zhim."

The imperator's tone made Madeline stiffen. "What's wrong?"

"The fight with the *dag'tar* is scheduled for tomorrow," Galen said. "The Srinar are stealthily selling tickets." Galen's gaze glittered. "We're out of time. We have to get them out tonight."

"The other houses?" Raiden asked.

Galen's jaw tightened. "Still deliberating. We go without them."

This was it. Tonight, they were freeing Blaine and the women.

Madeline looked at Lore, standing so straight and tall beside her. Her heart clenched. He hadn't argued about her coming this time. He was so handsome, and he was hers.

He'd forged a life for himself from the ashes of his past. He'd lost everything—his family, his way of life, his sister—but here, inside the walls of the arena, he'd made a new life for himself.

He hadn't wallowed in his misery, or cursed the things he couldn't change. At the same time, he'd also honored the memory of his lost sister.

Madeline knew it was time she did the same. The thought of her Jack still filled her with pain, and she knew it probably always would. Still, even if she did commit to making a life for herself here on Carthago, the mother in her would never give up hope of hearing her son's voice again. One day, somehow.

"Okay, time to move out," Galen said.

The gladiators were tense but focused, as they moved as a group toward the sewer entrance. Night had fallen over the city, and the busy streets gave way to the quieter, darker ones.

This time, she was prepared for the stench of the tanneries and the sewer. When they reached the sewer lake, Madeline's steps slowed.

She wasn't going to lie to herself and pretend that she wasn't afraid. If there'd been one mutated monster in the water, she was sure there were more. She rubbed her belly, touching wounds that were long healed.

Fingers gripped her shoulder and squeezed. She shot Lore a shaky smile. He read her so easily.

She entangled her fingers with his and, together, they moved across the walkway. There were no signs of movement in the water.

Soon, they were back on the ledge, looking down at the cells below. It was eerily quiet. No voices, no cries, no guards.

Galen gave his signal, with a wave of his hand. Kace and Saff moved forward, uncoiling the ropes they both held over their shoulders. Madeline watched Saff activate a small device, a metal pin firing into the rock, before she tied the rope off on the pin.

Saff and Kace attached the ropes to clips on their belts, and, on Galen's command, the two gladiators jumped over the edge, whizzing almost silently down to the lower level.

"Ready?" Lore asked Madeline, clipping onto the rope.

She swallowed. She'd never done anything like this before. With thoughts of Blaine and the women in her head, she nodded, and let Lore clip her on.

"We'll go together." He moved her to the edge.

She looked down, her stomach doing a slow somersault.

Without warning her, he stepped off the ledge, taking her with him.

Madeline bit her lip as they flew downward. Her heart leaped into her throat, her hair flying into her eyes. By the time their descent slowed, excitement had overtaken her.

Her boots touched rock, and then Lore was there, unclipping her from the rope. As the others zipped down, she looked around. Kace and Saff stood nearby, bodies taut and weapons up.

Soon, the rest of the gladiators were crowded around. Carefully and quietly, they moved toward the cells. Madeline's gaze zeroed in on the cell where she'd last seen Blaine.

They reached it and she hurried to the bars.

The cell was empty.

Her heart clenched. "He's not here." She hurried along the line of cells. They were all empty.

She reached the one where she'd last seen the women.

Empty.

"There's nobody here." Saff shook her head.

As Raiden and Galen talked quietly, Madeline paced, eventually ending up at the edge of the *dag'tar* pit. She looked down into the darkness, her gut cramping with fear and suspicion.

She picked up a large rock and dropped it into the darkness.

There were no snarls or growls, or sounds of movement. The beast wasn't there.

She spun. "The *dag'tar* isn't here."

Lore cursed—an unfamiliar alien word. "The fight isn't tomorrow. It's *tonight.*"

"Where?" Madeline spun around, looking at all the tunnel entrances leading out of the place. "Where the hell are they?"

"They can't have gone far," Galen said. "You can't move a *dag'tar* around without someone noticing." He eyed the walls. "They're here somewhere. Break into pairs and spread out."

Raiden and Harper disappeared down a tunnel. Thorin waved at Nero and the two big men moved into another tunnel. Saff and Kace took off at a jog.

Galen nodded at Madeline and Lore. "Go."

"You'll be alone," Madeline said.

"I'm always alone." Galen pointed at another

tunnel. "Go and find your friends. I'm going to make contact with the other imperators, and see if they can mobilize their fighters."

Lore grabbed Madeline's hand. They hurried into the tunnel, darkness enveloping them. Her pulse tripped. They had to find Blaine and the others before it was too late.

Lore clicked on a small light. There was nothing in the empty tunnel that gave any sign that anyone had passed this way. They moved deeper, taking several turns, when suddenly Lore's head shot up.

"You hear something?" She strained to hear anything.

"Voices."

He grabbed her arm and pulled her onward. Soon, she could hear the sounds, as well.

Cheering and excited shouts.

Madeline and Lore picked up speed. Ahead, light flickered at the end of the tunnel.

They slowed down and carefully crept out onto another narrow ledge. Madeline looked across the space, and her jaw tightened.

It was another circular sinkhole, but this one had been turned into a large fighting pit. Other ledges had been hewn into the rock to form seating, all of it lit up by burning torches attached to the walls. Below in the sand-covered pit, five tunnels were covered with huge metal gates. It was a makeshift underground arena.

"Drak," Lore spat.

She followed his gaze and went rigid. In the center of the fight pit stood a giant creature.

The *dag'tar* pawed the dirt slowly with its huge, clawed feet. Its overlarge arms dangled forward, knuckles dragging on the ground. It was covered in tangled brown fur, drool dripping from a large mouth that was still too small to contain its giant, serrated teeth. She also couldn't miss the huge, flaccid cock hanging between its legs.

Oh. My. God. It was so much worse than she'd imagined. The crowd was chanting, demanding to see the fighters.

Suddenly, on the ledge below, Madeline saw two Srinar guards carrying a struggling woman out between them. She was twisting and kicking, trying to break free. She was also hurling some interesting and creative insults at them.

She was tiny and had short, blonde hair that had probably been a neat pixie cut before her captivity. The guards held her at the edge of the pit.

This couldn't be happening. Madeline gripped Lore's hand, her nails digging into his skin. His gaze was glued to the woman, as well.

The *dag'tar* gave an ear-splitting roar. One of the guards stepped back, and they gave the blonde a shove.

She fell from the ledge, arms spinning. She hit the dirt in the fighting pit, landing on her hands and knees.

Madeline lunged forward. *No!*

***

Lore wrapped his arms around Madeline, listening to her harsh breathing as two other Earth women were dragged out of the tunnel where they'd been kept. Like their friend, they were pushed over the edge into the pit.

One was the tall brunette they'd seen earlier, and the other was a woman with hair as black as night.

How the hell could they help them? Lore scanned the cavern quickly and methodically, blocking out the cheering spectators, studying the fighting pit. A muscle ticked in his jaw as he counted the guards. There were a lot of them. Too many.

Below, the *dag'tar* roared. It was an aggressive and aggravated sound that echoed off the rocks around them.

The creature lumbered forward. Lore knew it might look slow and stupid, but he'd heard plenty of stories about them. When it suited them, they could build up a lot of speed, and they knew how to use their claws and teeth. Not to mention the fact that they usually tried to mate with their prey before they ate them.

The *dag'tar* pawed the dirt, sending up a spray of sand, and then suddenly rushed forward. Toward the women.

The tall brunette grabbed the other two, yanking them to the side. She waved and shouted, and they raced along the rock wall. The *dag'tar* pulled up before it hit the wall, stopping to sniff the ground where the women had been standing.

Between its legs, it now had a hard, giant erection rising up through the fur.

Lore watched the women warily backing away. Two stooped down to scoop up rocks, while the other moved with arms outstretched. He frowned. The black-haired woman's vision appeared to be impaired.

Rocks weren't very good weapons in this situation, but Lore knew what that sort of desperation felt like. The brunette paused, brushing a foot through the sandy ground. She snatched up something, and he saw it was a broken sword, with half the blade snapped off.

The animal roared again, and took a few steps in their direction. The women pelted it with rocks.

It charged. This time, the women scattered, ducking under its claws and running behind the creature. The brunette was dragging the blind woman beside her.

The *dag'tar* grunted, swiping out at them, but they scrambled out of the way. For now.

"We've got to get them out of there," Madeline said. "They won't be able to keep this up for long."

"Let's go that way." Lore pointed to rough steps carved into the rock wall. They appeared to lead down to the ledge below. The two guards who'd tossed the blonde woman into the pit were still standing there, their backs toward Lore and Madeline, their attention on the fight.

Madeline nodded and pulled out her laser sword. Lore pulled out his sword.

The crowd was far too busy watching the fight

below, to notice the pair of them creeping down to the next level.

"We can't miss the guards, or they'll send up a warning," he whispered to her. "You have to strike to kill."

Madeline nodded grimly. He was sorry to put her in this position, but the steady look on her face told him she'd do whatever she had to in order to save the women below.

"Remember our moves from training."

They moved fast, and gave the guards no warning. Lore stabbed his guard, and grabbed the man's lax body. Madeline had done exactly as ordered, and Lore snagged that guard as well. The Srinar was far too heavy for her to move.

He set them down against the rock wall, making it look like they were just sitting there, watching the fight.

In the pit below, he saw the *dag'tar* was getting closer and closer to the women, trapping them against the side of the pit. They were rapidly running out of options.

Lore grabbed a pouch off his belt. He watched, his muscles tense. When the creature charged the women, Lore pulled his arm back and tossed the pouch.

There was an explosion of black smoke around the creature's head. It roared, pounding the ground with its fists.

The women scrambled as far away from it as possible.

But seconds later, the *dag'tar* had recovered, its

large eyes once again focused hungrily on the women.

"Over here!"

The deep shout reverberated through the pit.

The crowd's screams rose to deafening levels.

Lore turned his head. Blaine Strong had entered the fighting pit from one of five gated tunnels. He brandished a sharp sword, his oil-slicked muscles gleaming in the firelight. One leather strap crossed his scarred, powerful chest.

"Now!" He bellowed at the women, waving a hand. "Behind me."

The trio moved as a group, sprinting toward him.

But the *dag'tar* heard and charged at them.

Blaine leaped into the air, hit the ground, and rolled...right under the *dag'tar*. With a massive thrust, he jammed his sword up into the animal's belly.

Orange blood splattered onto the sand, and the creature gave a shocked roar. Blaine rolled away.

Lore balanced on the edge of the pit, racking his brain. How could he help? And how could they drakking get them out without being mobbed by the guards? All while evading an enraged *dag'tar*?

Come on, Galen. Get down here, fast.

The *dag'tar* swung out a giant clawed arm. Blaine ducked and leaped to the side, tackling the black-haired woman out of the way. The brunette rolled through the dirt, pressing her belly flat to the ground.

But the small blonde woman wasn't fast enough.

The *dag'tar* caught her and she flew through the air. She hit the ground hard, tumbling through the sand several times before stopping.

The creature backed away from the others, and lumbered toward the fallen woman.

"Oh no," Madeline said, her voice tight. "Get up."

Lore watched, a knot in his belly, as the blonde struggled to push herself up. The woman was clearly dazed.

The *dag'tar* advanced. Madeline squeezed Lore's hand tight. Grinding his teeth together, Lore readied himself to jump, even though he knew he was on the wrong side of the pit, and too far away.

There was a clanking sound and Lore turned his head to see the gate on another tunnel into the pit open.

Suddenly, another big shape rushed out of the dark tunnel mouth.

A big, blue-skinned, tattooed alien ran forward, long, matted hair flying out behind him.

It was the beast-man.

With a roar of his own, the man leaped at the *dag'tar*. He yanked out two giant fighting forks that gleamed in the lights. He hit the *dag'tar*, driving the three-pronged weapons deep into the creature's side.

Then he leaped off, landing in a crouch right in front of the cornered woman.

The *dag'tar* spun in an unwieldy, frenzied circle, clearly in pain from its injuries. The beast-man approached the woman.

Drak. Lore's muscled locked tight. Was this blue

alien a friend or foe?

The woman looked up panicked, pressing against the rock wall. The beast-man moved closer, and grabbed her, pulling her up.

She was shaking her head. He pulled her closer and pressed his face against her neck.

"What's he doing to her?" Madeline frowned. "It looks like he's sniffing her."

But then the *dag'tar* let out a roar, louder than before. The spectators all gasped, a wave of unease rippling through the crowd.

It lumbered across the pit, its burning gaze on Blaine and the two women with him. It came ever closer, and soon it would be directly below Lore and Madeline.

It was now or never. "I'm going to jump onto the creature's back."

"Are you crazy?" she snapped.

"I have to get down there and help them. Go and find Galen." He didn't want her running off alone, but he really didn't want her in the pit.

But he also knew it had to be her choice. He knew his brave woman would do whatever she had to, in order to help the people below. Just as she'd sacrificed everything for her son.

Lore dragged in a breath. "Or you can come with me into the pit and help the women while I take down the *dag'tar*." Their gazes met. "Your choice."

He saw a smile flash on her lips, and something soft and bright flared in her eyes. Then her gaze zeroed back on the fighters and women trapped in the pit below, and her face hardened with resolve.

She gave a nod. "Don't die, Lore. I can't lose you, too."

He yanked her in for a fast kiss. "You too. Stay alive."

Then he grabbed her hand, spun, and leaped out onto the *dag'tar's* back, pulling Madeline with him.

Chapter Fifteen

Lore slammed onto the *dag'tar*'s back, holding on tight to Madeline.

Her eyes were wide, but she was calm and focused. He leaned over and, holding her hand, lowered her down to the ground.

"Get to the women." *And stay safe.*

She nodded, and a second later, she was sprinting toward Blaine and the other women.

Lore glanced at the blonde woman. She was still held protectively in the blue alien's arms, and he was walking toward Madeline and the other women. They were safe for the moment. Lore had to focus on taking down the *dag'tar*.

The crowd's wild shouts echoed in his ears, but he blocked them out. He lifted his sword, then brought it down, plunging it into the back of the animal's neck.

Orange blood splattered, and the creature reared, throwing Lore off. He landed on the dirt and rolled. When he came up, he saw Blaine standing beside him.

"The only way to kill it is to wear it down," he told Blaine.

The human nodded, and when Lore spotted

movement out of the corner of his eye, he saw the blue alien had joined them. He stared at Lore with golden eyes.

"Don't know if you can understand me," Lore said. "But the more cuts and wounds, the more it bleeds, the more likely we can get this thing down."

The *dag'tar* was staring at them now, thumping its claws on the ground.

"Don't let it pin you down," Lore added, spinning his sword. "You won't like the consequences."

The beast man didn't react, but Blaine gave him a nod.

Lore turned and charged. He ran in, ducking the animal's swing, and slashing at the creature's belly. Blaine was two steps behind him, hacking at the creature with his sword.

A second later, the blue alien landed on the *dag'tar's* back, jamming his fighting forks through the creature's fur.

Orange blood coated the sand, making it slick. Lore kept spinning, charging and slashing, working with the other two men. He couldn't see Madeline, but he assumed she and the women were staying out of range.

Suddenly, he heard shouts. He looked over and saw guards rushing down toward the fighting pit.

"Over here!" Madeline's voice rang across the pit.

He turned and saw the gates on a large tunnel slowly rising, the chains lifting it clanking as it rose. *Drak*. He suspected a whole bunch of Srinar guards were going to rush in at any minute.

Madeline sprinted toward the gate. She grabbed the chains, trying to keep the gate from opening. The other women rushed to help her.

The *dag'tar* swung a claw in Lore's direction. He reacted, just barely ducking beneath it. Then he had an idea.

He jammed his sword back in its scabbard on his side, and raced toward Madeline. He shouldered past her and grabbed the chain. He gave it a giant heave, trying to break it.

But the damn thing was strong. "Blaine!"

Blaine appeared and gripped the chain with him. The blue alien was busy keeping the *dag'tar* off them. Together, Lore and Blaine tugged, and the chain broke.

Lore lifted it. It was drakking heavy. "Lure him to me. I'm going to get this around his neck."

Madeline nodded. "You get ready. I'll bring him this way."

What? He'd meant *Blaine*. Before Lore could stop her, she turned and ran across the sand toward the *dag'tar*. She waved her arms at the creature.

"Over here, you big, ugly thing."

The *dag'tar* spun, sniffing the air. Its gaze zeroed in on Madeline, and it made a sound. It started lumbering toward her.

She walked backward, waving it closer. Then the animal picked up speed, each step getting faster and faster. Lore hefted the chain, getting it ready.

Madeline's eyes widened as the *dag'tar* ran at

her. She turned, sprinting toward Lore, her arms pumping.

The creature put on a burst of speed, faster than Lore had imagined possible. It tore after her.

Come on, dushla. *Faster.* Lore saw Blaine and the blue alien, trying to gain the beast's attention. But it had Madeline's scent now.

Lore focused on the chain, setting his ability free. He blocked out Madeline's scared face, and the boom of the animal's steps. He started to swing the chain over his head, around and around.

A little closer. Just a little closer. "Madeline! Drop!"

She dropped instantly to the dirt, throwing her arms over her head. The *dag'tar* thundered over her, and Lore flung the chain. It was glowing red-hot.

It wrapped around the creature's neck, burning into its fur and setting it alight.

The *dag'tar* stopped in its tracks, roaring and turning in a confused circle. It tried to tear at the chain, but its arms were too long.

Lore sprinted toward it. He leaped over Madeline, drawing his sword. He saw Blaine and the blue alien running in from the sides. The three of them charged together, skewering the *dag'tar* with their weapons—again and again and again.

The animal gave a wild cry and took one staggering step. Then it collapsed, the ground shaking, flames still flickering over its body. The stench of burning hair and flesh was overpowering.

Lore heaved in air, his lungs working like

bellows. He turned and saw Madeline on one knee, looking at him. She smiled.

She was covered in blood, sweat and dirt, and he'd never seen anything so beautiful.

Then behind her, he saw another gate open, and a wave of guards rushed in.

Lore ran, but the guards reached Madeline and the women before him.

Madeline fought hard, fists swinging, but a second later, one backhanded her and she dropped to the ground.

"No!" Lore yelled, attacking the Srinar guard closest to him.

Blaine streaked forward and attacked them, as well. The blue alien roared, rushing to attack the guards harassing the other three women.

"Stop!" A guard's voice rang out.

Lore lifted his head. He was holding a bedraggled Madeline in front of him, a sword pressed to her throat.

Lore froze, and sensed the others do the same. The other women were forced onto their knees.

"Drop your weapons," the guard said, no expression on his ugly, misshapen face.

Lore's fingers flexed on his sword.

The blue alien moved, but instantly, three guards rushed forward and jammed stun batons at him.

He fell to the ground, his body convulsing. The blonde woman let out a cry.

The guard with Madeline dragged her around, his sword biting into her skin.

Lore glanced at Blaine and cursed. Together, they dropped their weapons.

***

Madeline paced in the cell, working hard not to freak out.

She was back in a cage.

Maybe the walls weren't gleaming metal, or the ugly, skin-like substance she'd seen on the Thraxian ship, but the solid rock and bars didn't make her feel any better.

She was alone. A captive. Nothing.

She felt herself starting to hyperventilate, and forced herself to slow her breathing down. She was stronger than this. She was so afraid for Lore and the others. They'd dragged Lore away, fighting, and they'd shoved her in this cell just off the fighting pit.

She paced across the cell, turned, and paced back again. Galen, Raiden, Harper, and the others would be searching for them. She wouldn't be stuck here. They'd all be okay.

Dropping down onto her knees, she pressed a curled fist to her chest. Lore would be okay. She'd see him soon. Besides, she wasn't the weak, destroyed woman the Thraxians had captured. Now, she was stronger and had something to fight for. If no one came for her, she'd find a way out, herself.

She heard a rumble of voices outside, and suddenly, the cell door swung open. She leaped to her feet as two guards tossed Lore inside. He stumbled, and landed on his hands and knees.

The guards slammed the door closed again, and she raced over to Lore. When he lifted his face, her breath caught in her chest.

It was distended, and starting to bruise. One eye was swollen closed, and blood stained his mouth.

"Lore." The hyperventilating came back, her lungs so tight she couldn't get any air in.

His hands cupped her face. "Breathe."

"I'm fine. Fine." He was the one who was hurt, not her.

He pulled her close, sliding an arm around her. "You're not fine, and it's okay to admit that."

"You're hurt, and I'm stronger than this."

"I'm here for you, Madeline. No matter what. You don't have to be the strongest, or the one always in charge, or the one always with the answers."

She reached out, gently touching the one spot on his cheek that wasn't swollen or bruised. "It's the only thing I know."

"You see your vulnerability as a weakness. You haven't realized that I see it as the soft, lush part of the woman I'm in love with."

Love? Her throat was so tight. "Love frightens me, Lore. I'm no good at it. You're going to break my heart." And she'd never be able to pick up the pieces. It was already dented from what had happened to her, and Lore could shatter what was left of it.

"You have to give it to me first." His fingers

traced her cheekbones. "You have to trust me—" he broke off with a groan, bending forward.

Madeline slid her arm around him, lowering him to the floor. "Take it easy." God, what if he had internal bleeding? "We can have this conversation again when we get out of here."

He managed a nod. "The Srinar 'questioned' me. I think I convinced them we came alone."

Suddenly, the door swung open, a shaft of bright light spearing in on them.

Vashto stepped inside, arms crossed over his massive chest. He cast a molten glance at Lore. "You didn't have to sneak in. You could've asked, and I would've let you in the pit."

Madeline spotted Cerria behind the man, smirking at them.

"You're scum," Madeline spat at him. "Tossing innocent people in that pit."

Cerria pushed forward. "Chain the gladiator up and let me have him. I want him." She licked one of her claws, her gaze on Lore's chest.

"Sorry, love," Vashto said. "They want the fight ring this bad, I'm going to give it to them." He raked a look down Madeline's body. "It'll be a shame to watch you get torn apart."

Madeline's stomach turned over, her arm tightening on Lore.

Cerria laughed. "Well, that's not a bad consolation prize." The woman's smile was sharp. "Good luck."

"Screw you," Madeline said.

Vashto waved at the guards. "Bring them."

Madeline was torn away from Lore, and the guards dragged them out of the cell. She was half carried, half pushed down a tunnel, until they were both shoved out into the fight ring. A simple, dull sword was tossed at Lore's feet.

The *dag'tar's* body was gone, and fresh sand had been sprinkled over the floor. It didn't quite hide the blood stains.

The crowd stomped their feet, the sound like thunder in her ears. They'd been denied the carnage they'd been expecting, and now...they were out for blood.

She swallowed. Lore reached out and grabbed her hand. She saw he'd picked up the sword, testing its weight.

The tenor of the crowd changed. She and Lore turned and looked behind them.

The three women had been pushed into the pit with them.

Madeline hurried over to them. "Are you okay?"

The tall brunette with long, tangled, curly hair nodded. "I should be asking you that."

"We're still standing," Madeline said. "We came here to get you three and Blaine out. You're human."

The woman nodded. "And you're Madeline Cochran."

Madeline frowned. "Do I know you?"

The woman shook her head. "My name's Dayna Caplan. Former New York City Police detective. I'd just moved into security." She gestured to the black-haired woman. "This is Winter, she's a doctor."

Madeline saw that Winter's eyes were covered in a milky-white film.

"The Thraxians blinded her." Dayna's anger was tightly leashed. She waved at the tiny blonde. "And this is Mia, she's a spaceship pilot."

With a burst of clarity, Madeline realized who they were. "You were on the supply ship from Earth that was due at Fortuna Station."

Dayna nodded. "We saw the attack on the space station." The woman heaved in a breath. "They came after us next, and there was nothing we could do."

Madeline nodded. "Okay, well, everything's going to be okay. We're going to get out of here." She saw all the women darting looks at Lore. "And this is Lore."

The women stared at him. "He's...an alien," Dayna said.

"Yes, but I promise you, he's one of the good guys," Madeline said. "We're a long way from Earth. He's..." Madeline flicked her gaze up to his.

"Hers," he said. "I'm the man in love with her."

The other women were staring at Madeline with wide eyes. She took a deep breath and continued. "There are other humans here from Fortuna Station. We've found asylum with the gladiators of the House of Galen. It's safe, and the gladiators are helping us. We can talk more about this later, but right now, we need to find Blaine, and be ready to get out of here."

"How?" Dayna asked.

"The House of Galen will come," Lore told them.

Madeline prayed Galen and the others would be there soon. "Until then, we just need to stay alive."

The metallic, rattling clank of the gate echoed through the pit, and they all spun. The crowd started chanting anew.

"Stay back." Lore spun his borrowed sword, moving to stand in front of the women.

A familiar figure stepped out into the pit. The blue-skinned, tattooed alien with the long hair. The beast-man.

But when his hot, golden gaze hit them, a shiver ran down Madeline's spine. The beast-man's veins were popping out under his skin, the tendons in his neck strained.

He threw his head back, and let out an inhuman roar.

He didn't look anything like he had earlier. He watched them with no recognition.

The only thing in the beast's eyes was pure, animal fury.

What had they done to him? But Madeline didn't have a chance to think, because the alien started striding toward them, his fighting forks in hand.

Lore lifted his sword and moved to meet the beast.

Madeline's mouth went dry. She knew her protective gladiator would do anything to keep her safe. Including sacrifice his life.

Not going to happen.

Chapter Sixteen

Madeline pushed past Lore, but he threw out an arm, trying to hold her back.

"Madeline—"

She kept her gaze on the blue alien. "We're allies, remember?" The tattooed alien's eyes were on hers, and she swallowed hard. She saw no sign he knew them, just a wild, animalistic anger.

"Take care of the women," Lore said. "Find a way out."

The blue-skinned alien tensed, his gaze whipping back to Lore.

As Madeline stumbled back, she heard Mia the pilot let out a sob behind her. The sound seemed to infuriate the beast. He took a menacing step forward, and then charged at Lore.

Lore took a few running steps, and the men both leaped into the air.

They crashed into each other with a resounding smack, hitting hard.

Madeline watched, heart in her throat, as Lore and the beast pummeled each other. Lore swung with lethal power, opening up bleeding cuts on the beast's chest. She could tell he was trying not to kill the alien.

The blue beast roared his rage, getting in plenty of hard hits of his own, with his brutal fighting forks.

They were evenly matched. Madeline's hands curled into fists. She knew they'd go on and on, wearing each other down.

She didn't want the blue alien dead, but she wasn't letting Lore die here. She glanced over at the women. "We have to help Lore."

Madeline scanned the sand, and spotted something half buried nearby. A staff. She brushed the sand away and snatched up the metal rod.

The women flanked her, and they moved forward.

Madeline started to scream and shout, in an effort to distract the blue alien, and the other women joined in. As the beast-man spun around, Madeline swung the staff as hard as she could, slamming it into his back.

The blue beast let out a cry, stumbling forward. And that was just the advantage Lore needed.

Lore leaped onto the beast, driving him to the ground. He brought his sword down, skewering the alien through his shoulder.

"I don't want to kill you," Lore yelled. "Snap out of it."

But the alien heaved Lore off, leaping back to his feet. He aggressively circled Lore, preparing to attack again.

"Stop!" Mia ran in, her blonde hair a tangled mess around her face. "Please." She threw her hands up.

The alien went still, staring at her.

"Don't hurt him," Mia cried at Lore. "He helped me." She slowly stepped closer to the beast-man.

Madeline held her breath. Mia neared the alien, and pressed her hands to his chest. Lore stood nearby, chest heaving, his gaze never leaving the alien.

The crowd began to boo. They wanted fighting, and blood.

"Please, join us." Mia went up on her toes, the tips of her fingers brushing the beast's strong jaw. "We'll get you out of here."

Madeline bit her lip. If he lost it, he could kill Mia with one hard hit.

But then Madeline saw something amazing. The beast relaxed a little. His arms shot out and he grabbed Mia, dragging her into his chest.

Lore took a step forward, but Madeline grabbed his arm, shaking her head.

The blue alien took a deep breath, burying his face in Mia's hair. He was pulling in her scent, and something about the woman seemed to soothe him.

When he lifted his head, the wild look was slowly draining from his golden eyes. Then he looked at Lore, and gave a nod.

Madeline released the breath she'd been holding. Then suddenly, the crowd's booing silenced, and a roar pulsated through the seats.

God. What now?

The sound of rattling chains signaled the opening of another gate, and a new fighter stepped out into the pit.

She smiled. *Thank God.* It was Blaine.

"Blaine!"

Blaine raised his head, lifting twin swords as he did. Madeline's smile disappeared.

Like the beast, his muscles were straining, his veins standing out from his skin. And there was no shred of recognition or humanity in his dark eyes.

Inside, all she saw was a burning desire to fight and kill.

***

Lore stared hard at Blaine.

The man had been drugged. Lore recognized the signs. His chest was heaving, and he was fighting it, but Lore had heard about the kinds of drugs the Srinar used.

Blaine couldn't fight off the effects forever.

Where the hell was Galen? If the imperator and the other gladiators didn't get here soon, there'd be no one left to save.

Blaine's dark gaze stayed on Lore and the others, like a predator assessing its prey. It wouldn't be long before he attacked. Lore spun his sword around, adjusting his grip.

"Find a way out," he growled at Madeline.

With a nod, Madeline moved toward the others, gesturing at the rock walls.

He looked back at Blaine, his jaw tight. He knew it was a lost cause. This pit had been designed to keep well-trained and powerful fighters from escaping. What hope did the four Earth women have?

A tingle at the back of his neck made him look up. He saw Vashto and Cerria sitting on a ledge above, smiling down at them. Sand-sucking scum.

When he looked back at Blaine, that's when the man attacked.

The human hit with the force of a crashing spaceship.

Lore blocked the blows, his sword clashing with Blaine's. They moved across the sand, metal ringing on metal.

Drak, the man was strong. Lore didn't want to kill him. Blaine had already been through so much, and suffered far beyond what the women had. And Lore wasn't sure how Madeline, Harper, and the others would look at him if he killed their friend, even in his own defense.

"I'm not your enemy." Lore circled the man.

Blaine growled.

"Your friends are here to rescue you, Blaine."

Blaine rushed forward. Their swords hit, but Blaine swung his second blade in under Lore's arm, slicing open Lore's side.

Hissing, Lore spun away, ignoring the pain and the blood.

Using all his strength, he swung at Blaine. He fought hard, forcing the other man backward across the sand.

"Madeline and Harper are here," Lore called out in between each thrust of his sword. "Rory and Regan."

Blaine faltered for a second, before he screamed and swung his swords again.

"Harper," Lore said. "She's been looking for you."

Blaine stopped, staring at Lore. He shook his head, fighting against the drugs.

Then, with a loud roar, he charged forward again.

Lore danced back across the sand, blocking the fierce hits. *Drak*. He had to think of something else.

He was almost at the wall on the other side of the fighting pit. Then he remembered. The Srinar had taken his sword, but missed the tiny pouches tucked into his belt.

He snatched a pouch off his belt and tossed it at Blaine.

The red smoke exploded in the man's face, and Blaine started coughing and shaking his head.

Suddenly, a form came racing through the smoke toward Blaine. Lore's chest went hard. "Madeline, no!"

"It worked on the beast!" She ran right up to the enraged fighter. "Blaine! Please."

The man opened his eyes, staring down at her. Tears were streaming from his red-rimmed eyes.

"It's me, Madeline. Madeline Cochran." She held out a hand. "Let us help you."

"Let's give our champion of the fight rings a little help." Vashto's deep, gravelly voice interrupted them, his words echoing out across the fighting pit.

Lore cursed. What was the sand-sucking slime doing?

Another gate clanked open on the other side of the pit. Everyone standing on the sand stiffened.

At first, nothing happened, then it looked like shadows slinking out, detaching themselves from the darkness. Five giant shapes.

"Oktani fire wolves." Lore had never seen them before, had only ever heard of their viciousness.

The crowd cheered, watching the giant beasts with green, leathery skin move forward.

Suddenly, there was a scream from above. Lore looked up in time to see a man's flailing body falling, tattered clothes flapping around his body.

He landed hard in the sand in the center of the pack of wolves.

Now the crowd went quiet. The poor man got to his knees, terror lining his face.

Drakking hell. Lore started toward the poor soul, but one of the wolves leaped forward, opening its huge jaws.

A stream of fire poured out, engulfing the man.

The victim was turned to charcoal in seconds. The crowd went wild.

"Oh, my God." Madeline's face was pale.

But seeing the man die seemed to help Blaine fight off the worst of the drug's control. He was moving in front of the women, his swords held up, his gaze on the wolves.

Suddenly, the fire wolves howled, a haunting sound that echoed off the walls. One leaped forward with a giant bound. It landed, dirt spraying up from under its paws. It released a stream of fire in Madeline's direction.

PROTECTOR

Lore dived, knocking her off her feet. They rolled through the dirt.

He yanked her up and they turned. Blaine was hacking away at a wolf, dancing backward to stay out of the range of the vicious fire.

Behind Lore, the beast-man was standing in front of the other women, and facing off with another wolf.

The other animals were moving in closer. Lore ground his teeth together. They were all trapped with no way out.

He wrapped his arms around Madeline. He'd do anything to protect the woman in his arms. The woman who'd cracked open something inside him that he hadn't even known he'd buried away.

Staring at the fire wolves, he knew what he needed to do. He wasn't sure it would work, but it was worth the risk. Madeline was worth the risk.

He caught Blaine's gaze. Then Lore pushed Madeline into Blaine's hold.

The man wrapped his arms around her and she started, her gaze flying to Lore's. "What's going on?"

Lifting his sword, he turned to the wolves. "Only I can take them down." He breathed deep. He'd never had a chance to fully embrace his powers. He'd kept them hidden beneath illusions.

Now, it would be a trial by fire.

Literally.

He walked steadily toward the wolves.

"No!" Madeline screamed.

***

What was he doing? Her heart thundering in a bid to burst out of her chest, Madeline watched Lore walk into the center of the giant, wolf-like creatures.

They circled him, their eagerness visible in the excited lines of their bodies.

"Lore, no!" She tried to break free, but Blaine's strong arms held her back.

Lore turned, watching the animals. One leaped at him in a wild pounce. He slashed out quickly with his sword, skewering the beast.

As it fell on the dirt, dead, the rest of the pack went still and watchful.

"Kill him!" Vashto roared from above.

The wolves closed in on Lore. Madeline's breath caught in her throat.

All the remaining wolves opened their jaws, and let loose with wicked fire.

As the flames consumed Lore, savage pain cut through Madeline. *No.* She couldn't lose him. Not like this.

She'd survived her abduction, the loss of her son, the loss of everything that she'd held dear. But with Lore, she'd actually started living for the first time in her entire life.

And now her life was ending again.

The crowd was chanting, and tears streamed down her face. She never took her gaze off the hunched shape in the center of the red-gold fire.

Then she saw Lore straighten.

She gasped, shocked hope flaring. She heard Blaine's sharp intake of breath.

Lore lifted his arms, his body turning a glowing gold as he stood straight and tall. He moved his hands and a ball of flames grew between his palms.

Then he flung the fire back at the pack of wolves.

Amazing. Madeline smiled, as the crowd fell silent.

A wolf leaped forward, and Lore threw another ball of fire. He lunged and spun, sending streams of fire at the pack.

It was like some lethal fire dance. His grace and power stole Madeline's breath away.

Hers. This magnificent man, with so many layers and strengths, was all hers.

He threw one last ball of flames, and all the fire wolves were destroyed. Silence filled the fighting pit, Lore standing there, flames licking over his body.

"I want him!" Cerria screamed from the ledge above. "Bring him to me."

All the tunnel gates into the pit opened, and armored guards rushed in. They were all carrying nets.

Panic shot through Madeline's system. "We have to help him."

She broke free of Blaine's arms and ran forward. She heard Blaine cursing and running after her.

Several nets sprang over Lore and instantly burned up. He shot a stream of fire, and several guards fell, trying to slap out the flames engulfing them.

The next net slammed into Lore, and this time, it didn't burn.

This new net was made of metal wire. Madeline knocked into a guard, pushing him over. She saw Blaine fighting two other guards. But there were so many.

Another metal net crashed into Lore, tangling him up. He fell on the ground, struggling.

No. No one was taking him prisoner and keeping him in a cage. No way she was letting Cerria have him.

Madeline skidded down onto her knees beside Lore. The flames had died, but she saw all his veins were glowing gold beneath his skin. She grabbed the nets, wincing at the heat of them, and tugged.

Suddenly, she was wrenched backward. Her scalp burned with pain.

She twisted and saw Cerria's claws coiled in her hair. But the woman's hot gaze was on Lore, who glared back at her.

Cerria dragged Madeline up onto her feet. "This one is being sold off." Cerria shook Madeline. "I'm going to have Vashto send her off-world." An ugly, vicious smile. "Far out of your reach, gladiator. Then, you will be all mine."

Something in Madeline went very still. The thought of being sold again, being locked away... Fear burned like acid in her mouth.

Under the nets, she saw Lore's silver gaze ignite with flames. "I won't lose the woman I love to the likes of you." He pushed to his knees.

Suddenly, flames exploded all around Lore in a brilliant burst.

Chapter Seventeen

He wouldn't let it happen again.

Lore let the fire erupt out of him in a torrent. He'd lost Yelena. He wouldn't lose Madeline as well. She'd suffered enough, and he wouldn't let her suffer anymore.

Madeline was his—to protect, to cherish, to love.

The nets fell off him as charred rubble. He stood, and focused his fire on the nearby guards.

As a boy, he'd had basic instruction in using his abilities. All it required was a thought. But he hadn't completed his training as an adult, hadn't ever tested his control to the limit.

Now, however, he felt fully focused, the roar of the power humming through him.

He'd watched his family destroyed, his sister sold, the males of his species hunted to the ends of the galaxy. No longer.

He lifted his hands in front of him, a fireball forming between his palms. He threw it directly at Cerria.

As the fire engulfed the woman, she screamed. He expanded his ability to keep Madeline untouched by the flames. The fire bent around her, as though she stood in a protective bubble.

Her mouth was open as she stared at him.

Behind her, Cerria's remains fell to the ground.

Lore spun to attack the final guards...only to find them running for their lives.

He let the flames die, and strode toward Madeline. She just stared at him, and he couldn't read her face.

A tiny seed of doubt burrowed under Lore's skin, and his steps slowed. He couldn't tell if it was fear in her eyes... Then she ran and leaped into his arms, her arms and legs wrapping around him.

"Now that was a show," she said.

He pulled her in tight to him. "Don't ever be afraid of me."

"Never."

"I never used my ability to save Yelena. I didn't know how."

Madeline pressed her cheek to his. "She wouldn't have blamed you, *dushla*."

His heart clenched at her use of his endearment.

"We have company," Blaine said in a deep, rusty voice, interrupting the moment.

Lore lifted his head. Blaine, the beast-man, and women had closed in. They were staring at a new set of guards entering the fight ring. Lore looked up at Vashto in the stands. His face was a terrible mask, as he stared down at the spot where his lover had died.

"All guards to the ring," Vashto yelled. "Kill them. Kill them all!"

Lore set Madeline down, pushing her to the

center of their group. They were outnumbered, and without weapons.

"Turn the fire back on," Blaine said.

"I'm tapped out," Lore answered. He felt like he'd been running for days and his energy was low. "I'll do what I can."

The guards moved as a tight unit, holding up interlocking shields. These were trained fighters.

Suddenly, a large body leaped down from above and landed on the sand in a crouch in front of them.

Then the man stood, rising with a sword in hand. His tattoos were stark on his skin, and his red cloak flared out behind him.

Another man landed with a powerful grace, skidding on the sand, and raising his sword. His scarred face and icy gaze focused on the incoming guards.

"Raiden," Lore said with relief. "Galen. About drakking time."

A second later, Thorin's big body landed, followed by Harper and Nero. Kace and Saff hit the sand, both of them landing with graceful rolls.

Above them, other gladiators filled the ledges, chasing off guests and fighting the guards. Lore stared at the fighters, recognizing gladiators from other houses. All allies of the House of Galen.

"For honor and freedom!" Galen bellowed.

All around Lore, his friends lifted their weapons and their voices. "For honor and freedom!"

Lore looked at Madeline and raised his own weapon.

And for love.

***

Saff

As usual, Saff threw herself headlong into the fight.

Her muscles were practically vibrating, and with a determined smile, she swung her sword. With her other hand, she tossed her net device. It exploded outward, taking down two of the Srinar guards.

All around her, her fellow gladiators fought with shouts and focused determination.

A Srinar charged at her and she thrust her sword into him. She pulled back and spun to face another. She was filled with energy, the excitement of battle charging through her.

What happened down here in the fight rings was an abomination. And she was more than glad to play a part in taking it down.

She wrenched her blade out of another enemy just as a giant, blue, tattooed body rushed past her.

Drak. She watched as the wild man hammered into the line of guards with a fierce brutality. She made a mental note not to get on that guy's bad side.

Suddenly, the ground vibrated beneath her feet. She turned and saw a *gorgo* lumbering out of one of the gates.

She flashed a grim smile. *Good.* This fight hadn't

been challenging enough. The reptilian beasts were banned from the legitimate arena, since the taste of blood sent them into a feeding frenzy. Rory had once told her the creature resembled something from Earth called Godzilla.

The beast moved forward, and Saff raced toward it. It glanced her way, roared, and charged.

She dived, rolled, and came back up on her feet. She pivoted, watching the *gorgo* stomping its feet, turning around to come back at her again.

It started toward her, gathering speed, and Saff bounced on her feet, ready to attack.

A big male body rushed in front of her. She watched the man leap onto the creature and stab his sword into the *gorgo's* back.

He was stealing her kill!

It was the human man. *Blaine.*

She watched, peeved, as he stabbed the creature again. The *gorgo* spun around, enraged, and Blaine leaped off it, rolling on the sand and into a crouch.

Saff drew in a breath. She didn't care that the man was well-formed, with smooth skin the same shade as hers, and an interesting swirl of ink markings on his left shoulder. She didn't care that she liked the hard muscles and the intriguing scars that were marks of his skill in battle.

That creature was *her* prey.

She ignored the *gorgo* turning around and snarling, and stomped over to Blaine.

"That's my kill, Earth man."

Blaine rose, his gaze moving over her. Saff found herself snagged by dark, dark eyes filled with shifting nightmares.

"Only if you kill it first." His voice was a deep rumble.

He was challenging her? No one challenged Saff Essikani, the best net fighter in the Kor Magna Arena. She'd been proving herself her entire life. She didn't need some man from the other side of the galaxy questioning her skills and her right to a kill.

Spinning, she ran at the *gorgo*. She leaped into the air, landed on the beast's arm and started pulling herself upward.

She heard the Earth man's ripe curses. Suddenly, he jumped onto the *gorgo's* other arm, matching her pace.

Saff sped up, racing him to the top.

The confused *gorgo* tried to shake them off, and let out a stream of fire from its mouth, the heat searing. She kept climbing.

All of a sudden, the creature gave a violent shake. *Drak*. Saff lost her grip and went flying. Blaine's big body bumped into hers and they both landed in the sand.

They were both back on their feet in seconds. Blaine had lost his weapons. She saw the beast was eyeing the nearby group of human women.

Drakking hell. This wasn't a game anymore. The *gorgo* had to go down.

"It has a weak spot," she shouted at Blaine.

"Where?"

"The eyes. You distract it and I'll attack it."

She saw him gauging the creature's eyes. With a

nod, his muscles bunched as he readied to run in front of it.

"Human?" Before he even turned, she tossed him her spare sword. He caught it easily. "You might need this."

He lifted the sword, testing its weight. "Thanks."

Then, he raced toward the *gorgo*. She watched him as he ran, his speed and agility impressive for such a big man.

Saff forced her focus back on the creature. As Blaine yelled and danced around in front of the beast, she ran and leaped onto its back.

Seconds later, she crawled up behind its neck.

Down below, she saw Blaine darting in, slashing at the *gorgo*, and keeping it busy. It was completely ignoring her.

She changed her grip on her sword, leaned forward and jammed the blade into the monster's eye.

The *gorgo* reared back. Grimly, she held on and stabbed it again. This time, it jerked hard enough to knock her off.

Saff flew through the air, closing her eyes as she fell. *This was going to hurt.*

But instead of slamming into the dirt, strong arms caught her.

Her momentum knocked them both over and she landed on top of Blaine's big body.

Lifting her head, she stared down into dark eyes. She'd thought they were black, but up close, they were a very deep brown.

"Thanks," she said.

"Thanks for killing it."

"My pleasure, Blaine Strong of Earth." A part of her didn't want to move, but Saff pushed off his body. Standing, she dusted the dirt off her leathers. Around her, she saw her team had taken down all the remaining guards.

She held her hand down to Blaine. He slapped his hand into hers and got to his feet.

"You have the advantage," he said. "I don't know your name."

"Saff. Saff Essikani, gladiator of the House of Galen."

Blaine stood there, still holding her hand. "I hope I can see you fight again, Saff Essikani."

She tugged on her hand, but he didn't release it. "I live to fight, gladiator."

"I'm not a gladiator."

She smiled at him. "Not yet, but something tells me you will be." She tilted her head. "And you'd better let go of my hand, or I'll hurt you."

Something bright lit in his eyes, as though he was considering holding on to her longer.

"Blaine!" Suddenly, Harper ran in and slammed into Blaine.

The man wrapped his strong arms around his friend, emotion flooding his face. "Harper."

Saff stepped back.

But when she lifted her gaze, his dark eyes were watching her.

Chapter Eighteen

Madeline paced her office.

She'd already reorganized her shelves and drawers, and gone through every bit of paperwork. She shoved her hands through her hair. She'd run out of things to arrange and do.

She dropped into her chair. They'd come back to the House of Galen in the early hours of the morning, and, after making sure all of the wounded were being taken care of in Medical, she'd had a hot shower, then climbed into bed with Lore, and then dropped into a deep, dreamless sleep. She'd slept late, and when she'd woken, Lore had been missing.

Filled with energy, she'd worked for the afternoon in her office, but she still had a solid rock of emotion lodged in her belly. She realized that she'd been so focused on Blaine's rescue, that she'd been using that to block out the pain of missing Jack.

She squeezed her eyes closed. She felt...guilty. She was so relieved that Blaine and the women were free. She was pleased that Galen and his fellow imperators had shut down the Srinar's fight ring, at least for the time being. And she had finally admitted to herself that she was completely, and utterly, in love with Lore.

Here she was feeling happiness, when her son was so far away.

She heard someone at the door and looked up to see Galen watching her.

"The celebratory dinner has started," he said.

She gave him a nod. The staff had been busy all day, planning the dinner to celebrate the successful mission and welcome Blaine, Dayna, Mia, and Winter. "I'll make an appearance."

That one icy-blue eye watched her like a laser. "Are you okay? You should be happy. You helped free Blaine and the women. They're safe now."

Madeline nodded. "I am. What about the other man? The blue alien?"

Galen's face hardened. "We brought him with us, but then he became violent when we got back here. He's wild and unstable, and the healers are concerned that the drugs used on him may have caused some permanent damage."

"Has he said anything?"

"Not a word. For now, we have him as comfortable as possible in a cell."

Locked up. She hoped there was something they could do for him. "Have you seen Lore?"

Galen shook his head. "Not since this morning. He'll turn up."

It wasn't like Lore to just disappear. They'd survived that horrible experience in the fight pit together, and then this morning, he'd been gone. Madeline wasn't sure what to think.

Finally, she could make no more excuses. She made her way down toward the living area, where the dinner was being held. She stopped outside the door, listening to the happy chatter and laughter inside.

Everyone was celebrating, but she felt a little hollow.

For the first time in a long time, she felt very alone and she wanted Lore. That annoying prick of tears started, and she blinked them away.

Strong arms wrapped around her from behind. "Madeline."

And just like that, the riotous emotions inside her settled. Just the sound of Lore's voice steadied her. She hadn't realized just how much she needed him.

"Where have you been?" Her voice held the tiniest snap of anger.

"I had something I needed to do."

She turned and leaned into him. She felt him studying her face. Finally, he grabbed her hand. But instead of leading her into the dinner, he pulled her away from the living area.

"Where are we going?"

He didn't say anything until he pulled her into her office. He went straight to her couch, and pulled her into his lap.

"What's wrong, *dushla*?"

She sighed. "Am I that easy to read?"

"There is nothing I'd call easy about you." He stroked her cheek. "Tell me."

She shrugged. "I suddenly realized that I was

using the search for Blaine as a way to block my pain."

"And now that the search is over, the pain is back." His chin rubbed against the top of her head. "I'm here, Madeline. And it's okay for you to do whatever you need to, in order to get through the tough circumstances. It is okay to cry."

He was all solid strength, and always there for her.

Suddenly, Madeline couldn't hold back the tears anymore. The tears she really hadn't let herself cry. The sorrow poured out of her, sobs wracking her body. For herself. Her friends. For Jack. For Yelena.

Lore held her, brushing her hair back. "There you go. That'll make you feel better."

Slowly, the storm passed, and she looked up at him. She sniffled. "Maybe I feel a bit better, but I must look horrible."

He smiled. "A blotchy face and red eyes have never looked so beautiful."

God. Her heart clenched. She knew him well enough to know he meant every word. She was in love with this man. She—hardass Madeline Cochran—had fallen in love with a charming alien gladiator.

"Madeline? What's wrong?" His gaze turned serious.

"I was terrified of falling in love with you."

He watched her steadily, but his hands flexed on her.

"But now that I am," she said. "I couldn't

imagine my life without you."

"Thank the cosmos." Pure joy raced over Lore's face. He pulled her closer to him. "I love you too, *dushla*. So much."

He pressed his mouth to hers. The kiss was filled with so much love, tangled with desire.

He nipped at her lips. "I can never replace what you lost, Madeline, but I will spend every day helping you remember, and giving you something new to hold on to."

***

"Where are we going?" Madeline demanded.

Lore had her blindfolded, and was leading her by the hand. She'd told him she didn't like surprises, but she was smiling.

In the two weeks since they'd rescued Blaine and the other women, Madeline smiled a lot more. She was more relaxed, and was now an integral part of Galen's team, who looked after the smooth running of the House of Galen.

She'd started to make a life for herself at the House of Galen. With Lore.

The same couldn't be said for the others, yet.

Dayna, Mia, and Winter were trying hard to adjust, but were still dealing with the fact that there was no way back to Earth. Blaine was having withdrawal problems from the drugs the Srinar had used on him—he was moody and sticking to himself. Harper and Madeline were trying to help him, but it would take patience.

The tattooed beast was having the hardest time of all. The healers speculated he'd been placed in the fight rings as a young child. He'd been subjected to torture, fighting, and the drugs for years.

He was wild, and let no one close without lashing out. Galen wasn't letting anybody near him. Lore knew it broke Madeline's heart that the beast had to be locked up.

Lore knew time would help each of them, but sometimes, waiting and doing nothing was the hardest thing of all.

He led her into a building, and into an elevator. He pressed a button, and they whizzed upward. He was almost sorry that he'd blindfolded her, because he knew she'd enjoy the view out of the glass elevator at the city below.

"Tell me where?" she pleaded.

"You'll see."

The elevator stopped, and the doors opened. He led her out and took the blindfold off.

She blinked, her eyes focusing on the smiling man in front of them.

"Welcome to my domain," Zhim said.

She frowned at the information merchant, looking around the wide balcony of his penthouse apartment, and then to the dizzying view he had of Kor Magna, and the desert beyond.

"What's going on?" she demanded.

"You'll see." Lore tangled his fingers with hers. Zhim waved them inside.

His penthouse was all glass, clean lines, lovely

arches, and sparse furniture. But then he led them deeper and into a windowless room that was covered in comp screens.

This was Zhim's real domain.

He pushed a chair out and invited Madeline to sit. She did so gingerly.

"The gladiator here paid me a visit not long back and gave me a lot of money for your surprise," Zhim said.

She shot Lore a glance before frowning back at Zhim. "Why?"

"He became my investor a few weeks back. He sank a lot of money into my micro-wormhole technology." Zhim smiled and it was wide and pleased. "I'm happy to say that his investment is paying off. My early tests have been very successful."

Lore watched Madeline blink, confusion on her face. Then Zhim reached over to touch a screen. "I successfully sent some short, audio-only messages through a wormhole. And today, I received a response."

"Mom? I hope you're getting this?"

A young man's voice filtered through the speakers. Madeline stilled, her face turning white. She gasped, her fingers squeezing Lore's. His heart clenched for her.

"The message made it through telling us what happened and that you were okay. I was *so* happy to hear that you're alive. I can't believe you got abducted by aliens."

"Jack," she murmured.

Lore bit back a smile. The young man almost sounded excited.

"I miss you so much. Dad was pretty upset when he heard your space station had been attacked. But I just *knew* you weren't dead. Not sure how." Now he sounded a bit sheepish. "Anyway, it is so solar that you're getting to see the other side of the galaxy. I've been telling all my friends."

The young man paused to take a breath. Madeline pressed a fist to her mouth, unshed tears in her eyes.

"They're telling me I can't talk much longer. Take care. I miss you and I love you. I can't wait to hear your next message. Tell me everything about where you are. And next time, I'll tell you all about this girl." Jack's voice changed, turning a little shy. "Her name is Skye and I met her at school. Mom…I love you. Make sure you have fun where you are. You forget to do that sometimes. Okay, love you. Bye!"

Zhim shut off the message. Lore looked down at the tears streaming down Madeline's face.

"Thank you." She leaped to her feet and threw her arms around Lore. She buried her face against his chest. "I love you."

He hugged her tight.

Then she pulled back and moved to Zhim, pressing a kiss to the man's cheek. "Thank you, Zhim."

The information merchant cleared his throat. "I may give you a few discounts on the next messages."

She reached out and patted his arm. "And whatever you want to know about Earth, I'll tell you."

Zhim's eyes widened and he nodded. "I'm working on seeing how much data we can pass through the wormhole, and maybe including images as well. For now, it's just audio." He waggled his eyebrows. "I am good, though, so we'll see."

After they'd said their farewells, Lore led Madeline out onto the balcony. They leaned against the railing, staring out at the view of the setting suns. A warm wind ruffled her hair and Lore studied the look of contentment on her face.

"Happy?"

"So happy." She turned to him. "Lore, I'm not sure what I did to deserve you—"

"Just being you is enough. That's all you have to do. I have something else for you." He reached out, brushing the shell of her ear. He held out his hand.

It was a ring. It was made of a shiny, silver metal with a large, sparkling, blue stone in the center.

"It's beautiful," she said.

"Rory tells me it's called an engagement ring."

Madeline froze and her gaze flicked up to him.

"Breathe, *dushla*."

"You want to get married? Do you even get married here?"

"Joining, a show of commitment to the one you love. Yes, people do it here, and I want to, with you." He pulled out her left hand and slid the ring onto her finger. "I want to share my passion and fire with you. I want to love and protect you to my last breath."

"I want to love and protect you, too," she answered, smiling.

He smiled back at the woman from the other side of the galaxy who had captured his heart. "No illusions, no charm, just me and everything I have to offer you. If you'll take it."

Happy tears shimmered in her eyes. "Then it looks like we have a deal."

I hope you enjoyed Lore and Madeline's story! Galactic Gladiators continues with CHAMPION, starring human space marine Blaine Strong and tough, female gladiator Saff, and will be out late March 2017.

For more action romance, read on for a preview of Hell Squad: Marcus.

Don't miss out! For updates about new releases, action romance info, free books, and other fun stuff, sign up for my VIP mailing list and get your *free box set* containing three action-packed romances.

Visit here to get started:
www.annahackettbooks.com

FREE BOX SET DOWNLOAD

JOIN THE ACTION-PACKED ADVENTURE!

Formats: Kindle, ePub, PDF

Preview – Hell Squad: Marcus

READY FOR ANOTHER?

IN THE AFTERMATH OF AN ALIEN INVASION:

**HEROES WILL RISE...
WHEN THEY HAVE
SOMEONE TO LIVE FOR**

Her team was under attack.

Elle Milton pressed her fingers to her small earpiece. "Squad Six, you have seven more raptors inbound from the east." Her other hand gripped the edge of her comp screen, showing the enhanced drone feed.

She watched, her belly tight, as seven glowing red dots converged on the blue ones huddled together in the burned-out ruin of an office building in downtown Sydney. Each blue dot was a squad member and one of them was their leader.

"Marcus? Do you copy?" Elle fought to keep her voice calm. No way she'd let them hear her alarm.

"Roger that, Elle." Marcus' gravelly voice filled her ear. Along with the roar of laser fire. "We see them."

She sagged back in her chair. This was the worst part. Just sitting there knowing that Marcus and the others were fighting for their lives. In the six months she'd been comms officer for the squad, she'd worked hard to learn the ropes. But there were days she wished she was out there, aiming a gun and taking out as many alien raptors as she could.

You're not a soldier, Ellianna. No, she was a useless party-girl-turned-survivor. She watched as a red dot disappeared off the screen, then another, and another. She finally drew a breath. Marcus and his team were the experienced soldiers. She'd just be a big fat liability in the field.

But she was a damn good comms officer.

Just then, a new cluster of red dots appeared near the team. She tapped the screen, took a measurement. "Marcus! More raptors are en route. They're about one kilometer away. North." God, would these invading aliens ever leave them alone?

"Shit," Marcus bit out. Then he went silent.

She didn't know if he was thinking or fighting. She pictured his rugged, scarred face creased in thought as he formulated a plan.

Then his deep, rasping voice was back. "Elle, we need an escape route and an evac now. Shaw's been hit in the leg, Cruz is carrying him. We can't engage more raptors."

She tapped the screen rapidly, pulling up drone images and archived maps. *Escape route, escape route.* Her mind clicked through the options. She knew Shaw was taller and heavier than Cruz, but the armor they wore had slim-line exoskeletons built into them allowing the soldiers to lift heavier loads and run faster and longer than normal. She tapped the screen again. *Come on.* She needed somewhere safe for a Hawk quadcopter to set down and pick them up.

"Elle? We need it now!"

Just then her comp beeped. She looked at the image and saw a hazy patch of red appear in the broken shell of a nearby building. The heat sensor had detected something else down there. Something big.

Right next to the team.

She touched her ear. "Rex! Marcus, a rex has just woken up in the building beside you."

"Fuck! Get us out of here. Now."

Oh, God. Elle swallowed back bile. Images of rexes, with their huge, dinosaur-like bodies and mouths full of teeth, flashed in her head.

More laser fire ripped through her earpiece and she heard the wild roar of the awakening beast.

Block it out. She focused on the screen. Marcus needed her. The team needed her.

"Run past the rex." One hand curled into a tight fist, her nails cutting into her skin. "Go through its hiding place."

"Through its nest?" Marcus' voice was incredulous. "You know how territorial they are."

"It's the best way out. On the other side you'll find a railway tunnel. Head south along it about eight hundred meters, and you'll find an emergency exit ladder that you can take to the surface. I'll have a Hawk pick you up there."

A harsh expulsion of breath. "Okay, Elle. You've gotten us out of too many tight spots for me to doubt you now."

His words had heat creeping into her cheeks. His praise...it left her giddy. In her life BAI—before alien invasion—no one had valued her opinions. Her father, her mother, even her almost-fiancé, they'd all thought her nothing more than a pretty ornament. Hell, she *had* been a silly, pretty party girl.

And because she'd been inept, her parents were dead. Elle swallowed. A year had passed since that horrible night during the first wave of the alien attack, when their giant ships had appeared in the skies. Her parents had died that night, along with most of the world.

"Hell Squad, ready to go to hell?" Marcus called out.

"Hell, yeah!" the team responded. "The devil needs an ass-kicking!"

"Woo-hoo!" Another voice blasted through her headset, pulling her from the past. "Ellie, baby, this dirty alien's nest stinks like Cruz's socks. You should be here."

A smile tugged at Elle's lips. Shaw Baird always

knew how to ease the tension of a life-or-death situation.

"Oh, yeah, Hell Squad gets the best missions," Shaw added.

Elle watched the screen, her smile slipping. Everyone called Squad Six the Hell Squad. She was never quite sure if it was because they were hellions, or because they got sent into hell to do the toughest, dirtiest missions.

There was no doubt they were a bunch of rebels. Marcus had a rep for not following orders. Just the previous week, he'd led the squad in to destroy a raptor outpost but had detoured to rescue survivors huddled in an abandoned hospital that was under attack. At the debrief, the general's yelling had echoed through the entire base. Marcus, as always, had been silent.

"Shut up, Shaw, you moron." The deep female voice carried an edge.

Elle had decided there were two words that best described the only female soldier on Hell Squad— loner and tough. Claudia Frost was everything Elle wasn't. Elle cleared her throat. "Just get yourselves back to base."

As she listened to the team fight their way through the rex nest, she tapped in the command for one of the Hawk quadcopters to pick them up.

The line crackled. "Okay, Elle, we're through. Heading to the evac point."

Marcus' deep voice flowed over her and the tense muscles in her shoulders relaxed a fraction. They'd be back soon. They were okay. He was okay.

She pressed a finger to the blue dot leading the team. "The bird's en route, Marcus."

"Thanks. See you soon."

She watched on the screen as the large, black shadow of the Hawk hovered above the ground and the team boarded. The rex was headed in their direction, but they were already in the air.

Elle stood and ran her hands down her trousers. She shot a wry smile at the camouflage fabric. It felt like a dream to think that she'd ever owned a very expensive, designer wardrobe. And heels—God, how long had it been since she'd worn heels? These days, fatigues were all that hung in her closet. Well-worn ones, at that.

As she headed through the tunnels of the underground base toward the landing pads, she forced herself not to run. She'd see him—them—soon enough. She rounded a corner and almost collided with someone.

"General. Sorry, I wasn't watching where I was going."

"No problem, Elle." General Adam Holmes had a military-straight bearing he'd developed in the United Coalition Army and a head of dark hair with a brush of distinguished gray at his temples. He was classically handsome, and his eyes were a piercing blue. He was the top man in this last little outpost of humanity. "Squad Six on their way back?"

"Yes, sir." They fell into step.

"And they secured the map?"

God, Elle had almost forgotten about the map.

"Ah, yes. They got images of it just before they came under attack by raptors."

"Well, let's go welcome them home. That map might just be the key to the fate of mankind."

They stepped into the landing areas. Staff in various military uniforms and civilian clothes raced around. After the raptors had attacked, bringing all manner of vicious creatures with them to take over the Earth, what was left of mankind had banded together.

Whoever had survived now lived here in an underground base in the Blue Mountains, just west of Sydney, or in the other, similar outposts scattered across the planet. All arms of the United Coalition's military had been decimated. In the early days, many of the surviving soldiers had fought amongst themselves, trying to work out who outranked whom. But it didn't take long before General Holmes had unified everyone against the aliens. Most squads were a mix of ranks and experience, but the teams eventually worked themselves out. Most didn't even bother with titles and rank anymore.

Sirens blared, followed by the clang of metal. Huge doors overhead retracted into the roof.

A Hawk filled the opening, with its sleek gray body and four spinning rotors. It was near-silent, running on a small thermonuclear engine. It turned slowly as it descended to the landing pad.

Her team was home.

She threaded her hands together, her heart beating a little faster.

Marcus was home.

***

Marcus Steele wanted a shower and a beer.

Hot, sweaty and covered in raptor blood, he leaped down from the Hawk and waved at his team to follow. He kept a sharp eye on the medical team who raced out to tend to Shaw. Dr. Emerson Green was leading them, her white lab coat snapping around her curvy body. The blonde doctor caught his gaze and tossed him a salute.

Shaw was cursing and waving them off, but one look from Marcus and the lanky Australian sniper shut his mouth.

Marcus swung his laser carbine over his shoulder and scraped a hand down his face. Man, he'd kill for a hot shower. Of course, he'd have to settle for a cold one since they only allowed hot water for two hours in the morning in order to conserve energy. But maybe after that beer he'd feel human again.

"Well done, Squad Six." Holmes stepped forward. "Steele, I hear you got images of the map."

Holmes might piss Marcus off sometimes, but at least the guy always got straight to the point. He was a general to the bone and always looked spit and polish. Everything about him screamed money and a fancy education, so not surprisingly, he tended to rub the troops the wrong way.

Marcus pulled the small, clear comp chip from his pocket. "We got it."

Then he spotted her.

Shit. It was always a small kick in his chest. His gaze traveled up Elle Milton's slim figure, coming to rest on a face he could stare at all day. She wasn't very tall, but that didn't matter. Something about her high cheekbones, pale-blue eyes, full lips, and rain of chocolate-brown hair…it all worked for him. Perfectly. She was beautiful, kind, and far too good to be stuck in this crappy underground maze of tunnels, dressed in hand-me-down fatigues.

She raised a slim hand. Marcus shot her a small nod.

"Hey, Ellie-girl. Gonna give me a kiss?"

Shaw passed on an iono-stretcher hovering off the ground and Marcus gritted his teeth. The tall, blond sniper with his lazy charm and Aussie drawl was popular with the ladies. Shaw flashed his killer smile at Elle.

She smiled back, her blue eyes twinkling and Marcus' gut cramped.

Then she put one hand on her hip and gave the sniper a head-to-toe look. She shook her head. "I think you get enough kisses."

Marcus released the breath he didn't realize he was holding.

"See you later, Sarge." Zeke Jackson slapped Marcus on the back and strolled past. His usually-silent twin, Gabe, was beside him. The twins, both former Coalition Army Special Forces soldiers, were deadly in the field. Marcus was damned happy to have them on his squad.

"Howdy, Princess." Claudia shot Elle a smirk as she passed.

Elle rolled her eyes. "Claudia."

Cruz, Marcus' second-in-command and best friend from their days as Coalition Marines, stepped up beside Marcus and crossed his arms over his chest. He'd already pulled some of his lightweight body armor off, and the ink on his arms was on display.

The general nodded at Cruz before looking back at Marcus. "We need Shaw back up and running ASAP. If the raptor prisoner we interrogated is correct, that map shows one of the main raptor communications hubs." There was a blaze of excitement in the usually-stoic general's voice. "It links all their operations together."

Yeah, Marcus knew it was big. Destroy the hub, send the raptor operations into disarray.

The general continued. "As soon as the tech team can break the encryption on the chip and give us a location for the raptor comms hub—" his piercing gaze leveled on Marcus "—I want your team back out there to plant the bomb."

Marcus nodded. He knew if they destroyed the raptors' communications it gave humanity a fighting chance. A chance they desperately needed.

He traded a look with Cruz. Looked like they were going out to wade through raptor gore again sooner than anticipated.

Man, he really wanted that beer.

Then Marcus' gaze landed on Elle again. He didn't keep going out there for himself, or Holmes.

He went so people like Elle and the other civilian survivors had a chance. A chance to do more than simply survive.

"Shaw's wound is minor. Doc Emerson should have him good as new in an hour or so." Since the advent of the nano-meds, simple wounds could be healed in hours, rather than days and weeks. They carried a dose of the microscopic medical machines on every mission, but only for dire emergencies. The nano-meds had to be administered and monitored by professionals or they were just as likely to kill you from the inside than heal you.

General Holmes nodded. "Good."

Elle cleared her throat. "There's no telling how long it will take to break the encryption. I've been working with the tech team and even if they break it, we may not be able to translate it all. We're getting better at learning the raptor language but there are still huge amounts of it we don't yet understand."

Marcus' jaw tightened. There was always something. He knew Noah Kim—their resident genius computer specialist—and his geeks were good, but if they couldn't read the damn raptor language...

Holmes turned. "Steele, let your team have some downtime and be ready the minute Noah has anything."

"Yes, sir." As the general left, Marcus turned to Cruz. "Go get yourself a beer, Ramos."

"Don't need to tell me more than once, *amigo*. I would kill for some of my dad's tamales to go with it." Something sad flashed across a face all the women in the base mooned over, then he grimaced and a bone-deep weariness colored his words. "Need to wash the raptor off me, first." He tossed Marcus a casual salute, Elle a smile, and strode out.

Marcus frowned after his friend and absently started loosening his body armor.

Elle moved up beside him. "I can take the comp chip to Noah."

"Sure." He handed it to her. When her fingers brushed his he felt the warmth all the way through him. Hell, he had it bad. Thankfully, he still had his armor on or she'd see his cock tenting his pants.

"I'll come find you as soon as we have something." She glanced up at him. Smiled. "Are you going to rec night tonight? I hear Cruz might even play guitar for us."

The Friday-night gathering was a chance for everyone to blow off a bit of steam and drink too much homebrewed beer. And Cruz had an unreal talent with a guitar, although lately Marcus hadn't seen the man play too much.

Marcus usually made an appearance at these parties, then left early to head back to his room to study raptor movements or plan the squad's next missions. "Yeah, I'll be there."

"Great." She smiled. "I'll see you there, then." She hurried out clutching the chip.

He stared at the tunnel where she'd exited for a long while after she disappeared, and finally ripped his chest armor off. Ah, on second thought, maybe going to the rec night wasn't a great idea. Watching her pretty face and captivating smile would drive him crazy. He cursed under his breath. He really needed that cold shower.

As he left the landing pads, he reminded himself he should be thinking of the mission. Destroy the hub and kill more aliens. Rinse and repeat. Death and killing, that was about all he knew.

He breathed in and caught a faint trace of Elle's floral scent. She was clean and fresh and good. She always worried about them, always had a smile, and she was damned good at providing their comms and intel.

She was why he fought through the muck every day. So she could live and the goodness in her would survive. She deserved more than blood and death and killing.

And she sure as hell deserved more than a battled-scarred, bloodstained soldier.

Hell Squad

Marcus
Cruz
Gabe
Reed
Roth
Noah
Shaw
Holmes
Niko
Finn
Devlin

Also by Anna Hackett

Treasure Hunter Security
Undiscovered
Uncharted
Unexplored
Unfathomed

Galactic Gladiators
Gladiator
Warrior
Hero
Protector

Hell Squad
Marcus
Cruz
Gabe
Reed
Roth
Noah
Shaw
Holmes
Niko
Finn
Devlin

The Anomaly Series
Time Thief
Mind Raider
Soul Stealer
Salvation
Anomaly Series Box Set

The Phoenix Adventures
Among Galactic Ruins
At Star's End
In the Devil's Nebula
On a Rogue Planet
Beneath a Trojan Moon
Beyond Galaxy's Edge
On a Cyborg Planet
Return to Dark Earth
On a Barbarian World
Lost in Barbarian Space
Through Uncharted Space

Perma Series
Winter Fusion

The WindKeepers Series
Wind Kissed, Fire Bound
Taken by the South Wind
Tempting the West Wind
Defying the North Wind
Claiming the East Wind

Standalone Titles
Savage Dragon
Hunter's Surrender
One Night with the Wolf

Anthologies
A Galactic Holiday
Moonlight (UK only)
Vampire Hunter (UK only)
Awakening the Dragon (UK Only)

For more information visit AnnaHackettBooks.com

About the Author

I'm a USA Today bestselling author and I'm passionate about ***action romance***. I love stories that combine the thrill of falling in love with the excitement of action, danger and adventure. I'm a sucker for that moment when the team is walking in slow motion, shoulder-to-shoulder heading off into battle.

I write about people overcoming unbeatable odds and achieving seemingly impossible goals. I like to believe it's possible for all of us to do the same.

My books are mixture of action, adventure and sexy romance and they're recommended for anyone who enjoys fast-paced stories where the boy wins the girl at the end (or sometimes the girl wins the boy!)

For release dates, action romance info, free books, and other fun stuff, sign up for the latest news here:

Website: AnnaHackettBooks.com

Printed in Great Britain
by Amazon